JEAN LORRAH
COLLECTED

JEAN LORRAH COLLECTED
STORIES FROM SIX UNIVERSES

JEAN LORRAH
WITH LOIS WICKSTROM

EDITED BY
JACQUELINE LICHTENBERG

BORGO PRESS

JEAN LORRAH COLLECTED

"Pay The Piper" was first published in *Owlflight* No. 2, edited by Millea Kenin; Copyright © 1981 by Jean Lorrah. "Witch Fulfillment" was first published in *Hecate's Cauldron*, edited by Susan M. Shwartz; Copyright © 1982 by Jean Lorrah. "Sympathetic Magic" appears here for the first time; Copyright © 2007 by Jean Lorrah. "The Beholder" was first published in *Realms of Fantasy* #1 (October, 1994); Copyright © 1994 by Jean Lorrah. "The Rooster Under the Table" appears here for the first time; Copyright © 2007 by Jean Lorrah and Lois Wickstrom. "Change of Command"; Copyright © 2001 by Jean Lorrah. "Short Quarter"; Copyright © 2001 by Jean Lorrah.

CONTENTS

FOREWORD

As I sat down to write this foreword to the collection of my own short stories, I had just reread *Space Cadet* by Robert Heinlein for the first time in many years. The purpose of the rereading was to prepare to participate in a retrospective appreciation of that book at the 2006 World Science Fiction Convention in Los Angeles.

Rereading *Space Cadet* reminded me of why (*how* is a different story; this is the *why*) I became a science fiction reader and writer. I was eleven years old, and in the hot summer my family took me to visit cousins in Iowa. A city girl who lived with my nose in a book, I found farm life pretty uninteresting until my cousins took me to the one-room library in their small town. I absolutely pounced on the table of books for young readers, and would have grabbed a dozen had I been permitted.

But, "One book each," my aunt told us. So I chose a book with a subject I had never read about before: a book called *Space Cadet*.

It was the 1950s, before Sputnik was launched. There was no NASA. There was no astronaut program. There was no *Star Trek*. The closest I had ever come to reading about space was in a book about identifying the constellations.

Space Cadet was the most exciting book I had ever read — this for a girl who had already devoured not just Grimm but Andersen, all the many colors of Lang's fairy tale books, *The Three Musketeers* and all its sequels, *20,000 Leagues Under the Sea*, *The Time Machine*, and dozens of historical novels set in far off times and places.

I read to escape the gray day-to-day existence of life in a steel town, where my life consisted of working in the family grocery store and school, where I was socially challenged because I was not academically challenged. I read in order to be somewhere else.

What made *Space Cadet* more exciting to me than all the classics I had read? For the first time, I was reading about an exotic and exciting life I believed I could actually have. The nerdy kids in the book were not social outcasts — they were heroes. I felt I would actually fit into that world.

Furthermore, Heinlein wrote about the near future, using contemporary science. Never mind that I didn't understand a word of it; at age eleven I was certain that, like the boys in the story, by the time I graduated from high school I would.

What I took home from Iowa that summer changed my life. I knew how to look for more books by the author who had so stimulated my imagination. When I looked Heinlein up in the card catalogue in my city library at home, I was delighted to find that they had several of his books.

But when I went to the fiction shelves, not one of them was to be found. When I asked the librarian to reserve the missing books so that I could read them when they were returned, she found that most were not checked out. They were, in fact, shelved in an area I had never looked at before, called "Science Fiction." To my amazement, off in one corner there was a floor-to-ceiling bookcase filled with books that — remember, this was the 1950s — were almost all about going into space, living in space, or visiting or living on other planets.

I was in heaven! For the next several years I did not voluntarily read anything but science fiction. I consumed Asimov, Bradbury, and Clarke along with Heinlein, and never quite understood why Andre Norton's books felt more welcoming to me when "he" (I knew that Andre was French for Andrew) was clearly not (at that time) regarded as in the same league as the Big Four. For I quickly found and subscribed to some science fiction magazines, reading their editorials and reviews as Word from On High.

In the meantime, in fumbling adolescent fashion, I began to write the stories I could not find on the shelves or in the magazines: stories with female heroes. In fact, I had not even gotten through my first half-dozen sf books, mostly Heinlein juveniles, before I started to write a book with the classic title, *Girl in a Space Suit*.

Thankfully, the title is all I can remember about it today — but you have to understand that I was a preteen girl with no interest in Barbie or stories about nurses.

What YA literature offered me in those days was stories about boys and men doing things I was interested in, or girls and women doing things that bored me to tears. Why wouldn't I attempt to write about girls doing exciting, interesting things? So, while I loved all the science fiction I read, I felt left out. It was the 1950s; there was no women's movement, no "math without tears" class for girls. And I had no idea how far my father was ahead of his time when he took his daughter to work, right into the steel mill — there was no national day for it, and everyone just thought my family was strange, not least because they were saving to send a girl to college.

I was very lucky to be born into that family. While all the neighbors thought it was criminal that I was not sent to the vocational school with all the other "smart" girls, to learn shorthand, typing, and bookkeeping, my parents sent me to the regular high school because it had an academic track as well as gang rumbles and a championship football team. Most of the city knew only about the football team and the gangs.

Still, although I was definitely on the right educational track, high school was just as painful to me as to the average sf fan. So every moment that I could, I took refuge in reading. I read the works of the Golden Age as they were published, loving them and yet having that increasing sense of being left out. In older adolescence, not knowing that a thousand other girls were doing the same thing, I spontaneously invented the science fiction romance.

While I was in high school, Sputnik was launched, the U.S. and the Soviet Union began the space race, and my fellow students and I were told that there was a future in space for all of us. Even when I came to realize that the body I was dealt was never going to be athletic enough to allow me to be a pioneer, and the brain I was dealt was great with words but terrible with numbers, I remained certain that I would leave Earth. I changed my expectations to teaching literature in a school on Mars — or at the very least, at the Moon colony or a space station. The combination of moving on to college and New Wave science fiction ended my obsessive reading of the genre, except that I still devoured every new work by my favorite authors — the ones who never betrayed me by writing incomprehensible and depressing tales not even set in space. However, reading was no longer the only interesting part of my life — in college I found students of both sexes who enjoyed the same things I did, and developed a social life. When I was in graduate school, *Star Trek* exploded into our lives, and a whole new kind of fandom developed via — gasp! — snail mail.

I began to write for fanzines. I earned my doctorate. The U.S. went to the Moon. I was even more certain that before my teaching career was over I would teach somewhere other than on Earth. I continued in fandom, and began to sell professionally. Having published a number of nonfiction articles, I met Jacqueline Lichtenberg, who had just published her first professional novel, *House of Zeor*. That meeting ultimately resulted in my first professional publication of fiction being a novel, *First Channel*, in collaboration with Jacqueline, in the Sime-Gen universe that she had created.

She encouraged me to start my own series, and soon I had created the universe of *Savage Empire*. We were never bestselling authors, but we had a regular following, and in those days that was enough to be secure as a midlist author. For a decade, we were in the enviable position (along with several hundred other authors) of being able to publish virtually any book we wrote, individually or together. Those were the golden days of the healthy, hefty midlist, now sadly a thing of the past.

Teaching, of course, is the ideal profession for a midlist author: breaks of from two or three days to three or four weeks occur regularly through the school year, and the summer break provides a stretch of over two months for writing.

I was young and full of ideas, most of them book length. The one thing that frustrated me, though, was that despite all the contracts for novels, I could not sell my short stories.

Which brings me to the stories in this volume. The fact is, I'm not much of a short story writer. For one thing, I have always preferred reading character-driven stories over plot-driven stories, so naturally that is what I write. On average, it takes more words to develop character than plot.

But there are certainly writers who write successful character-driven short stories, so that is no excuse. The main reason I write at novel length is that that is the length of my favorite ideas. I very rarely come up with an idea that will fit into short-story length.

And that made it all the more frustrating that every time I took time from contracted novels to pursue an idea that so excited me that I was willing to write it on spec, it ended up wasting a lot of postage and finally reposing in the bottom drawer.

Such results did not encourage me to write at short length, but still the occasional story insisted on being written, and then, as I matured as a storyteller, they actually began to sell.

Note: what they don't tell you in creative writing classes is that it is much

harder to craft a good short story than a good novel.

Over my publishing career I have thus far written twenty-one novels and only eleven short stories. Furthermore, few of my short stories are really short. Most hover around the 10,000 word mark, and none is under 4000 words. Also, when I create a whole universe, I always find that there are many stories to tell in it, not just one. Thus even fewer of my short stories are standalones — most tend to be pieces of series.

This volume does not include my three Zhag-Tonyo stories from the Sime-Gen universe. Look for those in *Sime-Gen Collected*, which also includes stories by Jacqueline Lichtenberg.

Here, though, you will find stories that are part of other series: "Change of Command" and "Short Quarter" in my aborted attempt to write about traveling in space, and "The Beholder," part of the Witch Woman series that I intend to return to eventually. The first story in that series, "Human Voices," appeared in *Dragon* magazine, and later on the CD that collected all the early issues of the magazine.

The CD contract prohibits me from publishing the story elsewhere. So, "The Beholder" is the only Witch Woman story in this volume.

The old woman who narrates all the Witch Woman stories tells us of events from her past life. She is a kind of minor witch who knows herbs and a few spells, but does not have great magical power. She is also far wiser about other people than about herself. The witch woman serves her small village by the sea as herbalist, fortuneteller, healer, and a kind of unofficial love and marriage counselor. She helps others while remaining frustrated herself, and through her entire life she never manages to find lasting love. The closest she ever comes will be told one day in a novel entitled *True Love's Blood*.

As you might imagine from what I have told you of my childhood, I have always wanted to write about living and working in space. Ironically, *Star Trek*, with the same promise of a future for humankind in space that I had first found in *Space Cadet*, prevented me from doing so — at least professionally. You see, I loved *Star Trek*, wrote *Trek* fan stories, and then in the 1980s had the opportunity to write four professional *Trek* novels for Pocket Books.

Although out of print, there are many used copies, and they are also available in e-book form, so if you would like to read them they are easy to find: *The Vulcan Academy Murders* and *The I.D.I.C. Epidemic* in the Original Series and *Survivors* and *Metamorphosis* in Next Generation.

During that same time, with my *Savage Empire* series successful, I tried to begin a new series in short story format. *Savage Empire* is firmly grounded on an alternate Earth. I felt it was time at last to launch my own series of stories set in space. Knowing *Star Trek* inside out, I could not possibly accidentally recreate anything fans had already seen on screen. *Star Trek* and my space stories share nothing except the idea of humans and nonhumans working side by side, and such stories had been around for at least two generations before *Star Trek* hit the airwaves. If you recall, my very first science fiction inspiration, *Space Cadet*, concerns humans and aliens learning to cooperate to rescue the crew of a crashed spaceship. No way did that basic concept begin with *Star Trek*, nor did *Trek* have a monopoly on it.

There is nothing like Starfleet in my series — the ships are merchant ships serving a company, analogous to the East India or Hudson Bay companies of Earth's days of exploration by sea. They have some kind of FTL drive, but it doesn't break down or require dilithium crystals or any other hard to come by material to create plot complications. The aliens on board are about as far from Vulcans or Klingons as it is possible to get.

Still, I ended up writing only the two stories you see here, because no matter where I sent them, the rejection letter said the same thing: "Too much like *Star Trek*." I honestly believe that if I had not been associated with *Trek* through the Pocket novels, the stories would have been judged on their own merit and in the context of the entire history of science fiction rather than the fact that they took place on a starship, like a certain popular television show.

It hurt very badly that, after becoming a science fiction fan via *Space Cadet*, wanting to go into space, and intending to write stories about life in space, I am for all practical purposes banned from doing so. I am very happy that this project allows me to get these two stories into print at last.

*****

The other stories are standalones, and one of them — although professionally published — is a perfect example of the writer's rule, "An idea is not a story."

"Pay the Piper" is a very weak story built on a strong concept. It is one of my earliest stories and one of my earliest frustrations: I knew it had a good "what if" idea behind it, and could not at the time understand why it bounced and bounced and bounced before finally finding a home in a small-press magazine. Now I know it was lucky to find a home at all.

Teaching is a good way of really learning how to do something. Now that I have taught creative writing for years, when I reread that story I cringe. It's all tell-don't-show, while effective storytelling must be show-don't-tell. There is nothing wrong with the story I chose to tell — it's how the story is told, passively, with huge information dumps, that is all wrong. The only reason I've decided to include it is that it clearly demonstrates my growth as a writer.

I would certainly never write that (or any) story that way today. And by the way, if you are a frustrated writer who keeps coming up with great ideas and still having your stories rejected, chances are you are making the same mistakes I did. Great ideas are a dime a dozen. It's the craft of writing you must learn, to make those ideas come to life. Join a writing workshop, and if no one in it is able to suggest ways to make your stories better, drop out and join another.

There are numerous workshops online, including one that Jacqueline Lichtenberg and I run on simegen.com.

There is an old saying that when you are ready, the right teacher will appear. Once you have found the right workshop for you, and have begun selling your stories you might want to go back and look at what was taught in the ones that did you no good. You may be surprised to discover that they all taught the exact basics that you needed — it was a change in you, when you were ready, that brought about your breakthrough.

To return to the stories in this volume, the remaining two are experimental. "Sympathetic Magic" is horror, and "Witch Fulfillment," as you can tell from the title, is humor. I very rarely write either one. However, both stories do demonstrate my favorite short story theme of the power of artifice, most often exemplified as the power of language. It crops up in my novels from time to time, but in gathering these stories together I realized that it is found in every one of them.

It may not be so apparent in the two space stories, "Change of Command" and "Short Quarter," because I was never allowed to continue the series (unless I wanted to store the manuscripts in the bottom drawer in hopes that after my death someone would decide they were publishable after all), but the direction the story arc was headed was to include Vron's problems understanding his crew and Lyria's problems understanding Vron. You may not notice Vron's careful evasion of a direct question in the first story, but surely you will notice the opening scene of "Short Quarter," in which Edgar Wolfe translates what Lyria Melladin is really saying. She is deliberately manipulating language to tell the truth, but not the whole truth. Linguistic misunderstandings, accidental or deliberate, were intended as a staple of this series.

In the Witch Woman stories, language plays a huge role because magic is performed with words. A spell is called a spell because of the importance of every detail of its wording. The word "grammar" comes from "glamour" — spellcasting.

"Sympathetic Magic" is of course itself a magical term — it is the kind of magic in which the spellcaster does or symbolizes something which then is mimicked in real life by the object of the spell. In simplest terms, stick a pin in a voodoo doll, and the person represented by the doll feels pain.

But there are no voodoo dolls in this story — it is words that have power. Thus
the term "sympathetic" in the title becomes ironic, for the wielders of words of power are anything but.

And there you have it: my full collection of non-Sime-Gen short stories. I hope you find something to enjoy in each of them, even the weakest — perhaps you can use "Pay the Piper" as a cautionary tale, to remind you, if you are an aspiring writer, that an idea is only the barest beginning of a story.

If that story inspires you to say, "I can do better than that" good! Go for it! You might be surprised how often I said that about published stories when I first attempted to write professionally. Writing is a craft that you can study, and it is a lifelong journey. When you stop learning, it is time to die.

I have just retired, after teaching at every level from seventh grade to graduate school. I never did get to teach on Mars, on the moon, or on a space station, but perhaps, now that we are finally building the space station, some of my students will. In the meantime, I am not standing still — I am going forward. I have many more stories to write, and I am now engaged in learning a new form of writing: screenwriting. Does that mean you will see my stories at your local theater? I wish! And I mean that sincerely. It may seem absurd for someone old enough to retire to set out to learn a whole new craft. However, given today's studio productions, independent productions, pay channel movies, cable channel movies, direct to DVD movies, podcasting, and whatever else the techies have up their sleeves, there is a world of media out there in desperate need of material. If I can learn the craft, perhaps one day you will see my work on screen. Some screen, somewhere.

And in the meantime, yes, I will continue to write books, and perhaps the occasional short story. The project through which you have found this book is a chance to bring my older work, and that of many other professional writers, back into print. So the past meets up with the future, and the future is built upon the past.

The eleven-year-old girl who found an entire life direction by reading one book still lives inside me. I may not go into space myself, but some of my books will!

To find out what I am doing at any given time, what cons I will appear at, what books are available or in process, please visit:

www.jeanlorrah.com.

To keep up with all the Sime-Gen activity, please visit:

www.simegen.com.

— Jean Lorrah
March 2007

PAY THE PIPER

I knew Julie had returned, of course, but I never expected to hear from her. I couldn't help watching everything about her on the news, but she wasn't interviewed.

The Performers were shown as a group, arriving at the Houston facility looking rather weary. Well, who wouldn't, after light-years of travel? Their manager spoke for them — good old George Henderby. It had been his choice to take Julie instead of me . . . but that was ten years ago. I was long over my disappointment.

For Julie, though, the faster-than-light trip had been only a year. Perhaps she thought I held a grudge. Perhaps that was why her voice had sounded so hesitant, almost weak, over the phone.

The last thing I, thirty-year-old Emma Cordair, wanted now was to face still-twenty-something Julia Vorsak. Yet there had been something in her voice, something plaintive, when she said, "Please, Emmy.

I want to see you. I want to tell you . . . you should be glad George didn't choose you."

And, of course, there was curiosity. How could I resist hearing firsthand what it was like to travel to another solar system, to live for almost a year on another planet, to dance before audiences of aliens? How could they comprehend ballet, the Zorgs, so different from us?

Perhaps that was why they were so intrigued. Lumpy bovine creatures, they created the most magnificent music humankind had ever heard. It was as if their music was created for humans to dance to, and human dance forms designed for Zorg music. I had choreographed my first ballet to Zorg music — while Julie was away. I was prima ballerina and successful choreographer now. Did she know that?

Was that it? Was she feeling out whether she could rejoin the company? That would be strange . . . awkward. She was still younger generation, a brilliant new dancer who might or might not fulfill her potential. I was middle-generation now, fulfilling mine — possibly goaded to overachievement by Julie's having been chosen to represent the human race to the Zorgs.

Well, I'd soon know why she had called. I was meeting her for lunch at Georgio's.

I took my class that morning, then showered and put on a dress I had brought along for the occasion. For the first time in years, I was aware of the way my body looked, rather than how it performed.

If there is any woman intimate with the shape of her body, it's a dancer. All day long she studies it in mirrors; at times she studies it on video. Yet she never looks at what I was seeing this morning.

Too thin. Breastless. The roundness my slenderness had had ten years ago had given way to stringiness; my hips and thighs showed power, not curvaciousness. The softly draped skirt covered them, but the strongly delineated muscles of my calves showed my age. *Should have worn trousers.*

At least my hair was good, fluffing up after the shower into soft waves. Still, if one looked, several white hairs sprung from the traditional center part. My face looked old — ageless, I rather hoped, but certainly not fresh and young, especially after all the years of theatrical makeup. I wore nothing but mascara and lip gloss today — it was currently fashionable not to conceal the dark circles under my eyes.

I was ready, but it was too early. Julie wouldn't be at Georgio's for half an hour. Nervously, I looked around the dressing room, seeing things I hadn't consciously noticed for years. There was a picture of Julie and me together, both dressed as Giselle. We had alternated the role the season before she had been chosen for the Zorg cultural exchange. We had both created a sensation, and the publicists had exaggerated only slightly the rivalry between us.

We were both ambitious, and yet we were the best of friends.

How interchangeable we appeared in that old photo, so young, so almost featureless that beneath the exaggerated stage makeup it was nearly impossible to tell which Giselle was Julie and which was me.

Both were ghosts now — a bit of us captured, no longer existing, as if the camera had taken those girls to itself forever. Soon afterward, Julie had left Earth, while I took out my disappointment in renewed ambition, grasping the opportunity left by Julie's absence. I was dancer and choreographer now, and taught classes as well. It was almost as if I had lived out both our potential these past ten years!

Recalling my bitter disappointment when George chose Julie over me, I found myself wondering if I would want to be Julie now, ten years later. *But only a year for her,* I reminded myself. Still, she had returned to a world that no longer remembered her for herself, but only as one of the Performers. Her celebrity came from having been to the planet of the Zorgs, not from her talent.

The strange thing was . . . since their return, none of the Performers had performed. It was almost two months. George had been on the news and all the talk shows. Video of the Performers had been shown, but not the Performers themselves.

A chill went through me. It was still fifteen minutes early, but I no longer cared if I arrived at Georgio's before Julie. I had to see her at the first possible moment, to find out what she had to tell me.

Memory walked with me through the city streets. The Performers were Earth's very best dancers, singers, actors, even acrobats and comedians — but all young. The trip would be too stressful for anyone over thirty, the Zorgs had insisted. As the Zorgs had FTL and we didn't, there was some fear that they might not be returned as promised, but they had been.

But in what condition? Why were none of the Performers performing?

By the time I reached Georgio's I was running — but ballet training served me well. I was not even breathing hard. I composed myself, and entered the dark interior. As my eyes adjusted, I could barely make out a figure in the back booth, where Julie and I used to come to whisper our secrets.

Yes, like a ghost in the dim light, she was there. She hadn't changed — still young, still hazy around the edges as if photographed through gauze. Had her experience not changed her at all?

I thought she wouldn't know me, but her eyes fixed on mine at once, and as soon as I was close enough she said, "Emmy. Oh, it's so good to see you."

Her voice was loud enough, well modulated, and yet it seemed an echo of itself.

Was I ever that young, that unformed? Her face seemed devoid of character.

Is it sour grapes, I grilled myself, or is she really only blankly pretty instead of beautiful as I remember?

"Julie," I said, sitting down opposite her, "how are you? Have you adjusted yet to the changes while you were gone? What are your plans?"

"Plans? Oh," she shrugged and said vaguely, "I suppose . . . I'll find something to do. They paid us enough so I'll never have to work."

Never have to work? Who thought of dancing as work? It was life!

"But when will you dance again? I thought surely by now they'd have set up a concert for the Performers."

"No, IThat is, I don't know, Emmy. But you look

terrific. I . . . saw you in *Zorg Variations* last Friday. You were wonderful."

"You were there and you didn't come backstage? Oh, Julie, everyone would be so glad to see you!"

"I couldn't face them. Not now. It was after I saw what you did with the Zorg music that I thought . . . I can face you, Emmy."

Her youth made her seem childish, vapid. Was I like her nine years ago? The new kids in the company aren't, not even sixteen-year-old Billie.

"Face me? Julie, everyone wants to hear about your adventures!"

The waiter brought us each a gin and tonic. Julie stared into hers. "There were no . . . adventures. I danced. And everywhere we went on Zorg there were those recorders. Every performance. It's all on Zorg, Emmy. Just as their music is here for you, all our performances are there, for them."

"Well yes, of course," I said. "But when are you going to do something new?"

She was still staring into her untouched drink. "I can't," she said. "I've tried. It's gone."

"What do you mean? Julie, are you ill?"

"No, not ill. Emmy, you choreographed the *Zorg Variations*."

"Yes. You could dance it, Julie. You have the —"

"No!" She cut across my words, the first glimpse of her old spirit, but it faded immediately. "No, not anymore. It's all gone. It's all on Zorg."

"What are you talking about?" I demanded, although the chill truth was already creeping up my spine.

I had worked from the Zorg recordings, known

the life that poured from them to inspire me to create some of the most intricate dance ever seen on Earth. And the Zorgs had recorded Julie's dancing the same way, her inspiration. . . .

She was smiling faintly. I recognized the smile now. It was not the innocent smile of the very young, but of the very old. She knew I knew.

"Do you remember the stories," she said, "about primitive people who feared photographs or recordings were capturing their souls?"

I nodded.

"Perhaps we should have taken a lesson from them," Julie said. Her hand touched mine — cold. "I don't think George knew . . . but he chose right. You were the one who could create from the Zorg music, not me. It was worth it, Emmy. What I did will inspire Zorg composers. Their musicians will record music for Earth, to inspire those like you, the creators."

I couldn't find words to answer or comfort her. After a while she said, "I hated you, after I realized what had happened. And then . . . I saw what you had created out of the exchange."

She lifted her eyes then, and there was a triumph of certainty in them. "It will come back to us. They'll send more music, and you'll create more dances. You dance them well, Emmy, but in the future it won't have to be you, just as it won't be me anymore. The dance — that's the thing — the dance and the music. When I saw that, I knew. It's worth it. It's worth anything."

As I looked at her, burnt out in a year, and considered my own slower but inevitable oxidation, I knew she was right. The Zorgs had simply found a faster way to do what all artists do . . . the one thing, perhaps, that is truly worth the price.

WITCH FULFILLMENT

It wasn't until she was twenty-six that Mary Sue Clyatt took up witchcraft. No handsome prince, count, or even baron had come into her life. Not a single millionaire, nor chance to win one on a TV show. The books she read, the movies she saw, the television that played every moment she was home, all assured her that such men waited, ready to sweep sweet young girls into adventure and marriage.

At twenty-six she was no longer a sweet young girl. Still pure and innocent, she had a squint from reading and peering at her computer screen, an extra twenty pounds, acne, and oily hair from the Sara Lee, pizza, and ice cream which consoled her in lonely hours. One day she caught sight of herself in the full-length mirror.

"Good heavens!" she gasped. "What has become of me?"

Such an epiphany might, for other women, mean diet, exercise, and a good haircut. For Mary Sue it meant the end of hope. "I've grown old!" she wailed. "Romance heroines are from seventeen to twenty-four. I am obsolete!"

She drowned her sorrow in double lattes and furtively watched the men come and go in the advertising office where she worked. Which of them might be her prince, come too late?

Then one day she was fitting copy into an advertiser's template, when the logo seemed to jump out of the screen. RED DEVIL CHILI, surmounted by a saturnine face drawn in red. There were horns, a goatee, pointed ears — a stereotype, but for Mary Sue a revelation.

"I'll make a pact with the devil!" After all, she came from good Massachusetts stock — some of her ancestors from Salem.

Although her favorite books were adventures in which young women were swept into intrigue and in the final paragraphs into the hero's arms, she had come across the occasional pact-with-the-devil story. The hero or heroine always received youth and beauty, along with whatever else she sought.

Mary Sue knew her way around a search engine, and for this project she searched the library as well. She tried a few spells, getting a raise and a promotion by giving her immediate superior migraines, but it was romance, not a career, she wanted. The negative spells — migraines — seemed to work, while the positive spells — making herself irresistible to men — did not. So she set out to make that pact.

Within a few weeks she learned a great deal from the grimoires and satanic websites, including the danger she was in. The devil would do his best to trick her, to give her exactly what she asked but omit something crucial, like eternal youth for the woman who asked for immortality and spent eternity getting older and older and older —

Mary Sue shuddered over that example and determined to make no such mistake. She would accept the risk. After all, what did she have to lose?

"Your soul," said the devil when he rose up inside her carefully drawn magic circle warded with salt and iron and the symbols she had researched so diligently.

"*You* can have it," said Mary Sue, "*if* you agree to my terms. Eternal youth and beauty —"

"Ten years," interrupted the devil. He wasn't *the* devil, of course, merely *a* devil, and not a prepossessing one. He stank of sulfur, he had a wart on his nose, and he seemed bored. "Standard contract for love-starved females," he droned. "Youth and beauty for ten years, no more, no less."

"What happens at the end of ten years?" asked Mary Sue.

"You die. I get your soul." He snapped his fingers, and a tablet computer appeared in his hand. Mary Sue could see her name and the date, already filled in.

The cursor scrolled past a solid block of fine print and "youth and beauty" appeared in a blank. "Will that be all?" asked the devil through a yawn.

"No!" Mary Sue exclaimed. "If I only have ten years, I want to live like the heroines of romance novels. I want excitement, adventure, handsome men in love with me. Rich men. Noblemen."

The cursor raced along as she spoke. Mary Sue

remembered the devil's trickery and added, "I don't want to be hurt. No sweet/savage stuff."

"Excitement and adventure, but no pain," said the devil distastefully. "Very well. That should do it —"

"No, wait! You said I'll die. I don't want that to hurt, either, or make me ugly. I want to die beautifully, with people around me who love me, who will cry for the passing of such a young and beautiful — and good — woman."

The devil twitched his tail in irritation. "Is that it?"

Mary Sue peered at the screen. "Just make sure it's ten full years of excitement and adventure and love," she said. "I'm a witch now. I can conjure you up any time I'm not satisfied. Stop jittering — this is a formal conjuration. You can't leave until I give you license to depart."

"Everybody's a lawyer!" snorted the devil.

Mary Sue took the tablet PC, which could pass through the wards, although the devil could not. She squinted, eyes watering in the haze of smoke that had arrived with the devil. The part she had added was clear enough, but the boiler plate was in red against black, in some arcane font. But the parts she cared about were there.

"Sign in blood," instructed the devil.

"On a touch screen?"

The devil produced a quill pen. "Left ring finger," the devil instructed, but Mary Sue had already picked up her athame. She punctured the tip of her finger.

"Ouch!" she said. "It's not supposed to hurt. It's in the contract."

"You call that pain? Anyway, you haven't signed yet."

Mary Sue dipped the point of the quill in her blood, and signed on the tablet screen. The blood appeared to seep through the screen, producing her signature in red. "How do I get a copy?" she asked.

"Email," the devil replied.

Mariamne went to her desktop and called up her mail. Sure enough, there it was, an attachment on a message from legalese@hell.com. She dismissed the devil and turned on the lights. Except for the magic circle, her bedroom was the same as ever. Not even a whiff of sulfur remained. In the mirror she saw the same dumpy, squinty, acne-spotted woman she'd been before. *If I have to,* she told herself, *I'll conjure up that devil every night until he gives me what I want!*

*****

The next morning, as she stepped outside, two men clapped a cloth over Mary Sue's face. As she drew breath to scream, she smelled chemical fumes. She blacked out.

When she came to, she was in a hospital room, swathed in bandages. A woman sat by the bed. In an accent Mary Sue could not identify, she said, "Mary Sue Clyatt no longer exists. You are Mariamne Winchester, distant American cousin of the Duke of Verlona. If you play your cards right, you will be a very rich woman." She held up a photograph of a darkly handsome man, standing before a magnificent stone mansion. "Wouldn't you like to marry this man and live in this house, have servants and give balls, wear beautiful clothes, and spend summers on the Riviera?"

"Sure," said Mary Sue. "What's the catch?"

The Duke's father and the real Mariamne's guardians had arranged their marriage. The principals had not seen one another since Mariamne was ten and the Duke eighteen. Now, it seemed, Mariamne had run off with a ski instructor. The man would not be bought, and Mariamne told her family that though they might forcibly separate her from her lover, she adamantly refused to marry the Duke. Instead of "I do," she would say "No!"

"Oh, that's beautiful!" empathized Mary Sue. "But what has it to do with me?"

"The Duke doesn't know his bride has married someone else. Wellington Winchester, Mariamne's guardian, wants to join his financial interests with those of the Duke of Verlona, who owns some Mideast oil companies. The wedding will seal the merger. If you can convince the Duke you're Mariamne long enough to get him to sign, you get half a million dollars. After that you can divorce the Duke or stay with him, whichever you choose."

"But why me?" Mariamne asked.

"You have the right coloring, build, and blood type, and the right Boston accent. With a little painless surgery we can make you look like Mariamne's photograph — no one's going to check fingerprints or DNA. We'll train you and dress you — all you have to do is fool the Duke until you get him to the altar. Then you have half a million dollars — and the Duke, too, for all we care."

When her extreme makeover team was through, Mary Sue had the first stipulation in her pact with the devil: youth and beauty.

She stared into the mirror in delight. Her dirty blond hair had become deep gold, and curled charmingly about a face of radiant complexion. Her eyes no longer squinted — wide open, they were revealed as violet. She was beautifully dressed, impeccably groomed, and not a day over nineteen — the age of the runaway heiress.

Wellington Winchester took Mary Sue to the ancient estate of the Duke of Verlona. No one questioned her identity, least of all the dark, handsome Duke, who was smitten with her at once. They rode, swam, and played tennis together, and, just as she had yearned to do, Mary Sue fell deeply in love. So deeply that she could not let the Duke, whose given name was Ricardo, marry a false bride.

Knowing she would lose everything, she sought Ricardo out on the eve of their wedding and, tears trembling on the edges of her lashes, confessed. Then she turned to leave.

Ricardo caught her arm. "Mariamne!" he said in a choked voice, and drew her to his chest. "I don't care who you are — you will always be my Mariamne, the only woman I have ever loved — the woman I am going to marry!" And he cut off her protest with a rapturous kiss.

As time passed, Mary Sue — now officially Mariamne, Duchess of Verlona — began to realize why her favorite novels always ended with a rapturous kiss. She was happy enough at first, honeymooning in Paris, gambling in Monte Carlo, skiing in the Alps — but eventually her delight cooled. Ricardo's hot Mediterranean passion didn't, though, and Mariamne took to having frequent headaches. For a time, Ricardo brought wet towels for her forehead, and sat holding her hand. Eventually, though, he left her alone.

They traveled to England for fox hunting. The day of the Hunt Ball the men rode while the ladies slept late and spent the day making themselves beautiful. It took little work for Mariamne; the youth and beauty part of her pact was certainly fulfilled. "But what about the love and adventure?" she pouted. "I think it's about time to call up that devil again!"

Just then she heard horses galloping outside, a great to-do. It was too early for the hunt to return —

She hurried downstairs just in time to see Ricardo being carried into the hall, his neck broken from a fall from his horse.

Although Mariamne could not inherit Ricardo's estate, which went to the next male of Verlona blood, she was left a very rich widow. She took rooms on the Riviera and went for long walks on the beach, trying to conjure up a proper attitude of mourning and convince herself that among her mixed emotions there wasn't really . . . a feeling of relief.

For two months she lost herself in the romantic novels she had always loved. Then she remembered that she had only a little more than eight years left for love and adventure, and began taking meals in the dining room. She sat alone at a table for two — as did a tall, distinguished gentleman who always looked distant and sad. Discreet inquiries brought information that he, too, was recently widowed. A wealthy English businessman, Peter Knightly.

One evening Mariamne arrived late, having

spent the afternoon shopping for something to catch Peter Knightly's eye. The dining room was full. The *maître d'* turned from assigning Mr. Knightly to the last table for two, and began to apologize to Madame the Duchess for not having reserved her a table — he had not expected a crowd — thought she had gone out for the evening —

Peter Knightly rose gallantly and offered to share his table. Mariamne found him intelligent, well educated, wont to quote poetry . . . a tragic hero with beautiful sad gray eyes. Peter was not the tennis-swimming-skiing type Ricardo had been. He gave Mariamne a delicious sense of being worshipped from afar.

In two weeks they were married, and Peter took Mariamne to his estate, called Wonderly, a formal, imposing house, strictly ruled by a housekeeper. Mrs. Cross was a pinched and harried woman who lived up to her name.

If it were not for Mrs. Cross, Mariamne thought, life with Peter would be perfect. They often went up to London for Peter's business. They would go out to dinner and the theater, and spend the night at the Ritz. Only away from Wonderly did Peter make love to her. He was gentle and hesitant, not demanding as Ricardo had been. Mariamne almost enjoyed it.

What she did enjoy was trying to pry out of Peter the tragic secret of his past. She knew it had something to do with his first wife, Ruth, but Mariamne could not get Peter to talk about her. The secret lay at Wonderly, for while his temperament was normally placid, at Wonderly he could easily be provoked into flares of temper.

It occurred to Mariamne that Mrs. Cross's insistence that the house be kept exactly as it was in Ruth's day was not good for Peter or his second marriage. So she decided to redecorate, choosing color schemes, mentally dismissing the uglier furnishings while considering what would blend beautifully with the many classic antiques. One thing that had to go was the collection of stuffed animals.

She was having a grand time until she came to a door which none of her keys fit. As she tried a second time, Mrs. Cross came sweeping down the hall.

"So!" said the housekeeper, "you want to know why your so-called husband cannot love you? He was married to a blessed saint, that's why. How dare you violate her sanctuary?"

Mariamne reminded herself that Mrs. Cross was only the housekeeper. "This is my house now," she said, pulling herself up to her full height. "If you don't like it, you can leave. But before you do, give me the key to this room."

The housekeeper's eyes darted lightning. "*Your* house? It can never be yours! Never!" She tugged at a chain about her neck, drawing a key from the depths of her bosom. "This is Mrs. Knightly's house — Mrs. *Ruth* Knightly's. Look upon the beauty she created, and see why you are nothing but a pale intruder!"

Mrs. Cross unlocked the door and flung it open. Mariamne followed her into a bedroom at least three times the size of her own. Although it was clean, it smelled funny, musty, unpleasant.

The huge canopied bed was set on a platform, its

hangings closed. Mrs. Cross opened the drapes, and sunlight flooded a room decorated in velvet and satin, white and gold. The dressing table sparkled with crystal. A comb, brush, and mirror of gold lay as if waiting for their owner. On the table beside the chaise longue was a bestselling novel from a year ago, a gold bookmark in it.

On the wall where light from the windows would strike it was Ruth's portrait. She was a dark beauty with huge eyes in a pale, angular face, black hair swept severely back, accentuating the perfection of her features. She was dressed in deep red, a color Mariamne could never wear.

"You see?" said Mrs. Cross. "How could the Master love a pale nothing like you, after such perfection?"

Mariamne glanced to the mirror to reassure herself of her own pink and gold beauty. "I'm sure Peter did love Ruth," she said, "and you did, too. But Ruth is dead. Peter loves me."

"Dead?" shrieked the housekeeper. "That's what the police said, but they never found her, did they? She could never leave Wonderly! It's hers, forever!" And she flung open the hangings on the canopied bed.

On the bed a shadowed form lay as if sleeping atop the white satin spread, wearing a deep red dress. In horrified fascination, Mariamne saw that it was Ruth Knightly — or her preserved, mummified remains —

Mariamne's screams brought Peter up the stairs at a run. "Oh, my God!" he gasped. He caught Mariamne protectively into his arms as he shouted at

Mrs. Cross, "It was you! It wasn't an accident! You killed her!"

"*You* killed her!" Mrs. Cross screamed back. "You tried to drive her from Wonderly!" She turned and ran as Peter held Mariamne like a drowning man clutching a life preserver.

Mariamne remained certain through the trial that her husband was innocent. He and Ruth, it seemed, had been childhood sweethearts. They married young, to the great joy of their families and the community . . . but as the years passed, they grew apart. Peter spent more time on business, while Ruth was often away from Wonderly, to the dismay of Mrs. Cross, who had come to Wonderly with Ruth.

One day, Peter testified, Ruth announced that she was leaving him. He told her to go ahead — he was better off without an unfaithful wife. She went upstairs to pack. The last time he saw her was at tea, when she taunted him about being so "civilized" about the end of their marriage. "But then you always were a cold fish."

After that, it had been thought, Ruth drove off. It was raining; she was agitated. In the morning her car was discovered at the bottom of the cliff. Her body was never found.

Now, though, the autopsy showed that Ruth had died of poison. Peter must have murdered her, pushed her car over the cliff, and then embalmed her body in the cellar of Wonderly, where he had done taxidermy as a boy. The half-mad Mrs. Cross might have been an accomplice, or simply a pitiful creature whose delusions Peter had used to his own ends. Mrs. Cross had disappeared the day Mariamne and Peter were shown Ruth's body. The prosecutor suggested that Peter might have murdered her, too.

Mariamne knew with all her heart and soul that Peter was no murderer. That did not affect the verdict: guilty.

Mariamne was too upset to drive home alone, so a police matron drove her back to Wonderly. What would she think, Mariamne wondered, if she knew that tonight at midnight *I'm going to conjure up a devil and give him a piece of my mind?*

But she didn't have to summon the devil. There was a light in one of the upstairs rooms when they drove up. "That's Ruth's bedroom!" Mariamne recognized.

The two women dashed up the stairs. Mrs. Cross stood before Ruth's portrait, holding a flaming candelabra. "They took you from me twice," she was saying. "I never meant to hurt you, my darling. *He* would have driven you away — you, the only true Mistress of Wonderly. *He* was supposed to drink the poisoned tea! I put the poisoned cup before him — if only you had not come in at just that moment. If he had drunk from it first! But he gave you that cup and rang for a fresh one. When I came in and saw — ! Then I realized it was fated. You were never to grow old, to lose your beauty. I preserved it, in the Master's old laboratory. And while he was away, I put you here, where you belong, never dreaming he dared desecrate your memory by bringing that — that —"

"That's enough, Mrs. Cross," said the police matron. "I arrest you for the murder of Ruth Knightly."

Mrs. Cross shrieked as she turned to the two women. She stared at Mariamne. "You!" she sputtered. "You dare! You'll never take her place!" And she swept the flaming candles against the drapes, then the bed hangings. The roar almost drowned the housekeeper's hysterical laughter. A wall of flame rose between her and the two women. The police matron tried to reach Mrs. Cross, was driven back by the flames, took one look at the way the dry timbers of the ancient house were going up, and hustled Mariamne out to the car, where she radioed for help.

By the time the fire department arrived, Wonderly was gutted. Peter was philosophical. "I couldn't stand to live there anymore. Now I'm free, my love. I'm not responsible for Ruth's death — not even as I thought I was for letting her leave in such anger. You've exorcized my ghosts, Mariamne!"

And Mariamne had a bit of news to cheer him further: "We're going to have a baby!"

Her pregnancy was easy; any time she began feeling uncomfortable, she would think, *Time to call that devil up again!* and her discomfort would disappear. Even her labor was rapid — and then she and Peter had a daughter. They named the child Victoria, and doted on her. Though she had a nanny, Peter and Mariamne would often walk her themselves through the parks of London, where they now lived.

Mariamne was supremely happy. She loved her baby and her husband, and the house just off Berkeley Square. She did wish that Peter would not pester her about a brother for Vicky when she had just got her figure back — but she could put up with love-making occasionally. While she loved to cuddle, she still did not care for the particulars required to conceive a child. But that was a minor matter, and did not serve to cloud her happiness.

Then, when Victoria was eighteen months old, Peter dropped dead of a heart attack. This time Mariamne did conjure up her devil.

"You've broken the contract!" she accused, her lovely eyes swollen with genuine grief. "I was supposed to have ten full years of love and happiness! There are almost six years to go, and my life is ruined!"

"Reread your contract, my dear," said the devil. "It doesn't say love and happiness. It says love and adventure and excitement. It's over two years since you had the kind of adventure and excitement appropriate to heroines of romantic novels."

"But I don't *want* that anymore!" Mariamne wailed. "I want Peter!"

"What's in the contract is what we will provide."

In despair, Mariamne joined the demi-monde of gamblers in Monte Carlo. There she met a Greek tycoon who quickly became fascinated by the beautiful young widow. He was old enough to be her father, and he adored Vicky.

Mariamne had enough money never to have to worry — but Plato Parnassus moved in a world in which yachts were given as tips to servants, and no one thought in any terms smaller than millions. Plato assured Mariamne that he understood she would never love him like the lost love of her life — but the place he offered her as his wife was too appealing to refuse.

But to Mariamne's horror, once he was her husband, the old man who had never done more than kiss her hand expected sex. Expected it morning, noon, and night, in bed, in the swimming pool, and in the courtyard under the Mediterranean moon.

Nor was he put off by headaches, "Sexual tension," he assured her. "Best cure is a glass of champagne and a good lay!" And he lowered his gross, hairy body over hers once again.

Fortunately, when they had been married only seven months, Plato jetted off on a business trip, to Mariamne's relief at the thought of a whole week without his demands. His Learjet crashed in the Caucasus Mountains, and Mariamne was a widow for the third time.

She decided she would never marry again. She was fabulously wealthy. Platoons of secretaries and accountants cared for her finances, while she cared for Victoria.

Mariamne vacationed in Italy when Victoria was four — and there the little girl was kidnapped. Alfonso Martini, the Italian police captain on the case, insisted that paying the ransom would not assure the child's safety. Mariamne tagged along with Alfonso on the trail, which led to a car chase through the mountains and a shootout at the hideaway — but Victoria was rescued unharmed.

In relief and gratitude, Mariamne had a brief affair with Alfonso — but the passion of gratitude quickly faded. He was a poor man, but proud. She tried to give him money, a house, a car, but he would have none of it. He did, however, take her to the orphanage in which he had been raised. Mariamne donated money to repair the old buildings, add several new ones, and set up a scholarship trust for all the children.

The gratitude of the nuns and children stirred new feelings in Mariamne, and she set out to distribute more of her wealth in worthy causes. She went into earthquake and disaster areas, and became famous as a modern Lady Bountiful. Doctors, administrators, volunteer workers — every man she met fell in love with her, but she touched their lives and moved on. Young, beautiful, loved by all, and yet untouchable — Mariamne was happier than ever.

It was more than nine years since Mariamne had made her pact. Victoria was going on seven. One day Mariamne found that she did not want to get out of bed.

Her doctors insisted there was nothing wrong but overwork, but when fatigue persisted they sent her to a clinic in Massachusetts — the first time she had been back in her home state since she had become Mariamne.

Several doctors worked on her case, but she was officially in the care of Dr. Stanley Welton, Jr., a young genius who believed in holistic medicine, and thus fell wholly in love with Mariamne. He found the cause of her debilitating weakness: a rare disease she could have contracted only on one of her missions of mercy to the tropics. There was no cure. She would simply weaken until she died, without pain.

And without losing her beauty, she saw in the mirror. As she grew pale, her eyes seemed huge. Her hair remained glossy and thick, and even on the days when she could not find the strength to put on makeup, she looked ethereal, her bonds with life already tenuous.

Stanley spent many hours in her room, and stretched hospital rules so that Victoria could visit her mother. Her little girl was Mariamne's only regret — her will guaranteed the child the best schools, all material needs, but who would be mother or father to her?

She told her worries to Stanley, and he in turn unburdened his heart about his father, a businessman who had expected his only son to run the family's corporate empire. When Stanley applied to medical school, his father disowned him.

Without Stanley's knowledge, Mariamne sent for Stanley Welton, Sr. As she was probably the only woman in the world who was richer than he was, he answered her summons. She introduced him to Victoria, who was showing signs of becoming as beautiful as her mother, and then sent the child from the room.

"Mr. Welton," Mariamne began, "you probably thought I sent for you to discuss some financial dealing. I didn't. I called you to show you an emotional investment that I am losing: my child. You have a child, Mr. Welton, though you deny him. I'm dying, but my child is at my side, and has every moment of my love that I can give her. When you die, Mr. Welton, will your son be at your side?"

Within a few minutes, Mariamne had Stanley Welton, Sr. reduced to tears and promises to make up with his son. In the midst of that, however, Stanley burst into the room, his eyes flashing fire. "How dare you?" he demanded of Mariamne. "What gives you the right to interfere between my father and me?"

"Stanley," choked out Stanley, Sr., "this gives her the right — son," and he clasped the young doctor into a hug so awkward that Mariamne wondered if he'd ever done it before.

So father and son were reunited, and Stanley found even more reason to love Mariamne, who now had only a few more days. "Mariamne," he told her, "I want to marry you. I can adopt Victoria, and she will have a father and a grandfather to love and care for her. But most of all, I want you as my own, even just for these few days."

So they were married — and six days later Mariamne died, her daughter weeping on one side of the bed, and the Stanleys, Jr. and Sr., weeping on the other as the muzak played a lilting minor-key melody. Then she was in hell, face to face with her devil.

Hell, at first glance, did not seem such a terrible place. She was in a room whose only light was a fireplace. A huge bed was heaped with cushions. She was naked, she realized, her hands automatically assuming the Venus-on-the-half-shell position as suspicion stirred at the back of her mind as to what her eternal punishment would be.

The devil laughed. "Welcome to eternity, Mary Sue Clyatt. Did you ever make out the fine print in our contract for modern love-starved females?"

As she shook her head, the devil grinned, and three forms approached out of the shadows. Three naked men: Ricardo, Peter, Plato! Mariamne backed off, gritting her teeth with the knowledge that, her contract fulfilled, she must now accept her punishment.

"Others will join you later, my dear," said the devil, "after they die. All those men, all madly in love with you —" Mariamne cringed, but the devil took no notice, "— but with one small difference, you see. For ten years you got all you wanted, any time you wanted. You modern *Sex and the City* females. You liberated women. Sex, sex, sex, eh? Just try to relieve your frustrations now, my dear! This is what it said in the fine print!"

He waved his hand, and the fire flared, penetrating the shadows that had hidden all their private parts. Mariamne stared. The three men *had* no private parts! She stared down at herself...feltIt was true! They were, every one of them, as featureless as Barbie and Ken dolls!

The men reached for her as the devil howled with laughter. "Mariamne!" "My beloved!" "My one true love!" She was held, caressed, smothered in kisses, pulled down onto the bed in a tangle of limbs — but nothing more could happen — ever!

It was an adolescent girl's dream come true: an eternity of cuddling and kissing with devoted men, without ever having to put up with sex. Mariamne laughed joyfully, and surfaced long enough to inform the disgruntled devil, "I never was a sex-starved liberated woman! All I ever wanted was love. Thanks for fulfilling the contract, though — 'cause if this is hell, don't you ever try to make me go to heaven!"

SYMPATHETIC MAGIC

"The word 'glamour'," said the young teaching assistant, "is another form of the word 'grammar'." Some of her students tittered, but she continued doggedly, "Can anyone explain the connection between the two words?"

She looked out over the students, a night extension class in the city. Supposedly, these people enrolled in Freshman Composition because they were interested in learning, unlike the students she taught on campus. After a semester of vacuous eighteen-year-old business majors, who considered spelling and grammar a function of one's word processor, she had been glad to get this assignment.

She had expected secretaries and housewives seeking to liberate themselves through education. Instead, she faced forty uncommunicative faces, thirty-two of them male, twenty-eight of them black. Even the three white women did not appear to have anything in common with her twenty-two years of middle-class upbringing.

A hand went up. The teacher gave a quick nod in its direction, relieved that someone was willing to speak, and met dark eyes in a smirking tanned face. Shaggy black hair framed his features. He needed a shave. *No,* she told herself crossly, *he cared enough to come here straight from his work.*

"The connection is," the man said, his small black eyes gleaming wickedly, "our grammar teacher thinks she's glamorous!"

Despite her furious blush, as soon as the laughter died down the teacher proceeded with her prepared lecture, acknowledging the student's comment only by saying, "This is a composition course, not a grammar course. However, grammar is the proper use and organization of words, and you can easily see how that applies to writing. Glamour, although we now think of it as merely an exotic attractiveness, originally meant magic or witchcraft. And magic is the power of words. That's what this course is about: power through words."

A black man raised his hand. He was bulky — a linebacker if she'd ever seen one. "My grand-mother do magic," he said. "She tol' me 'bout her granmamma, best conjure woman on the bayou. Done *gris-gris*, voodoo. They say she had Words of Power."

The teacher could hear the capital letters. While this was not exactly what she had planned for her lesson, the class turned to the big black man with obvious interest. They were alert. She could not let that die.

"You're absolutely right," she said. "Voodoo is done through the power of suggestion — the power of words. Unfortunately, that power can be misused. Take advertising —"

She steered carefully away from suggesting that the man's ancestors had misused their power, and soon had the class involved in a lively discussion of Superbowl commercials.

*****

The old woman hated winter. Her neighborhood market cut prices on bread and produce the last hour of Wednesday business, as fresh supplies came in Thursday morning. But the store didn't close till nine, and it was cold and dark out by eight — had been dark for nearly three hours. She would have to walk both directions in the dark.

At least tonight there was no ice or snow. It was the first nice Wednesday evening in weeks — late January masquerading as early March. A false promise of warmth, really just the absence of bone-penetrating cold, animated the exhaust fumes.

Before she left the building, she checked her mailbox in the foyer. It had been jimmied so often that the door would pop open to a sharp blow, even from her arthritic hand. She debated, assuming watchers in the shadows, if it were better to let them see how easily the mailbox opened, or into which pocket she replaced her keys. Finally she decided it was better to protect the royalty check potentially hidden inside. Any thief bold enough to attack her in person would have no compunction about searching her pockets.

The mailbox was empty. No check again today. She wasn't sure . . . were those fresh scratches? Had a check been stolen?

Did anyone still owe her royalties? Her agent had dropped her two years ago, after she had sold nothing new for five years before that.

She couldn't recall how long it was since the last time she had received a check. A year? How excited she had been that day, to find an envelope from one of her publishers! After months, maybe years, of neglect.

The check had been for $32.15 — royalties, the statement informed her, on a reprint of the French edition of one of her books. So she was still being read in France, even if America had forgotten her. She was remembered in America only by the computer that deposited her social security each month.

She clutched her coat tightly as she left the shelter of the foyer, a reflex after the string of cold, windy Wednesdays. Tonight the air was mild — comparatively. She wore woolen stockings, and a heavy sweater over the two-piece wool business suit beneath her shapeless overcoat.

The suit was long out of fashion — the last one she had needed for editorial conferences and autograph parties — but it was warm. She was able to lift her head, breathe the air without paining her lungs. Enjoying the brief respite from winter's storms, she set off briskly toward the market.

*****

In the pale/bright fluorescent light, the composition class proceeded. The teacher was pleased. The man who had teased her about thinking herself glamorous turned out to be the useful sort of student who would try to answer every question, breaking the ice so that others dared suggest more constructive answers. His jokes were frequent, but as often at his own expense as at hers. His name was Hiram Ramirez. She began to like him.

She began to like the whole class. She had been right: they were interested in learning, and although she heard the dialect that she knew would translate in writing into endingless verbs and fragmented sentences, she also heard sound common sense born of a street experience she had never known. *I, too, will learn in this class.*

After talking about the paper they were to write for next week's class meeting, she ended, "And now I'd like to get to know you a little better. Before you leave, please write something for me, no more than a page —" At the hint of bristling resentment, she quickly added, "It won't be graded. I want to know what you're hoping to learn in this course. Anything reasonable, I'll try to incorporate it into the lessons."

She passed out sheets of paper, having correctly guessed that most of them would come to the first lesson with no more than a small pad to take notes on. She had not anticipated the lack of pens or pencils — but those who had them shared, and the papers slowly piled up on her desk.

> i want lern fill out emplomint form.
> I hop you test not to hard.
> My husband thinks Im dumb to spend money on this class, but I told him its my money, my mother gave it to me for my birthday.
> What you said about words being Power. If I can learn to write and spell good, next time I'll take the computer class. Then I can get good job sted of cleaning towlets.

The teacher smiled. There was a motivation that would never occur to her sorority girls!

It was nine o'clock. Class was officially over. A flurry of papers landed on her desk, and the students headed out into the night. Two men and a woman remained in studious concentration.

Not wanting to appear impatient, but not wanting to miss the 9:15 bus either, the teacher said, "Please finish up and give me what you've written. This is not a graded assignment. I just want to know what you're looking for in this course."

The woman immediately signed her name to her paper and turned it in. One of the men got up and walked slowly forward, rereading his paper. When he got to the teacher's desk, he put the paper down on it to sign his name.

The big black man who had spoken about voodoo remained in his seat, his paper folded before him. When the other man finally left, he rose slowly from the desk that seemed a child's chair to his bulk, expanding like a genie out of a bottle, tall as well as broad.

The teacher stood her ground, gathering up the papers, reaching for his, anxious to hurry for the bus. It wasn't so cold tonight, but she still did not want to stand on the street for half an hour, till the next bus.

But the man withheld his paper. "I dunno," he said seriously. "Maybe I shouldn't take this course."

Resisting the thought that it would mean one less paper to grade, the teacher asked neutrally, "Why not?"

"My great-great-granmamma, she got nuthin'

but trouble from her power."

"Oh, but we're not doing voodoo," said the teacher, trying to hide her dismay. "That was only one example out of many. I wouldn't have thought of it myself. And besides, voodoo has much more to it than words. What we're doing here —"

"You teach us to write. She know how to write — back when it against the law for niggers read and write. It give her great power, strong power. Ever'-body come her for *gris-gris*. You know *gris-gris*?"

Fascinated in spite of herself, the teacher said, "An evil spell."

"Right. Granma Sordy, she take off *gris-gris*. She good Christian woman. Other voodoos, they mad at her, she take off they power. They make *gris-gris* on her."

"But it didn't work, did it? She must have understood the psychology."

The man had no use for psychological explanations. "It don' work 'cause she have protection. You know magic? My grandma tell me, you got protection, someone do *gris-gris* on you, it bounce right back on them."

"Yes," said the teacher. "Evil to him who evil thinks. But you won't think evil, or write evil, so —"

"Grandma Sordy, they burn her." The man's eyes looked into hers as if looking into flames. "After while, she think ever'body do *gris-gris* on her, so she make protection against ever'body. She write in her book, people sick. People have accident. People die."

"People believed that what she wrote would happen," explained the teacher. "Illiterate people —"

"How they know what she write?" the man demanded. Then he shrugged, turning back into an ordinary bluecollar worker in jeans and an army jacket. "No, I know you don' teach voodoo, ma'am. But I want power. I want be foreman."

"That we can help you with," said the teacher, smiling a bit too brightly in her relief. "Does a foreman on your job have to write reports?" She gathered her books and the students' papers into her briefcase, encouraging the man to walk outside with her.

On the street she felt more comfortable, more normal, as he talked about his work on an assembly line. But as they rounded the corner, her bus was pulling away from the stop. "Damn!" she said, running a few hopeless paces after it. "Now I'll have to wait for half an hour!"

As she came to a dejected halt, the black man said, "It's my fault. Come on — I drive you home."

"Oh, no — I live clear on the other side of town, out by the university."

The man frowned, and the teacher was suddenly apprehensive, alone on the street with him. When her eyes flickered right and left, looking for potential help, he asked, "You afraid to get in a car with me?"

"Why no," she began unconvincingly. "It's just that I can't ask you —"

"Lady, you *smart* not to ride with me!" he replied. "You don' know me — but you don' know this neighborhood, neither. You not safe alone here. I'll stay till the bus come."

"Uh . . . thank you," she said, blushing again. "I'm sorry. I didn't mean —"

"I tol' you: don' trust nobody, this part of town.

Not unless you got protection. You think you got Words of Power work on muggers?"

"I don't think muggers give their victims time for words. Thank you. I'd appreciate your staying."

*****

The supermarket was hot and stuffy, crowded with people still wearing the heavy coats appropriate to yesterday. The old woman joined a slow checkout line that trailed back into one of the aisles. She leaned wearily on her cart, glancing at the nearby rack of magazines, tabloids, and paperback books.

No longer did she scan the displays eagerly, looking for her own books and articles. No one wanted tightly knit mysteries anymore. Her agent had tried to get her to make the transition to violent, sexy thrillers. "You're not Agatha Christie," he'd told her. "You can't go on writing the same old thing and keep an audience."

But she had. Her name had been sufficiently well known to tempt smaller presses . . . for a while. But eventually her books stopped earning out, advances went down . . . and then the contracts stopped.

Her agent dropped her. She went back to stories and articles, but the neatly typed return envelopes — she had never learned to use a computer — reappeared in her mailbox so quickly that it seemed the post office must exchange the envelopes without their ever passing over an editor's desk. Finally she let them pile up, unopened.

As she stood waiting for the line to move forward, her eyes roamed over the bright covers of paperback books. Here was the sort of thing people wanted to read today. *Sordid Saturday*: a young girl ventures into the streets of Chicago in search of her drug-addict brother, and finds a night of abuse and defilement. *Knife of Passion*: a cult of devil-worshippers torture children, finally murdering them and drinking their blood. *City Heat*: a rapist strangles his victims with black lace garter belts.

Her stomach churned. How could anyone read such trash, let alone write it? She turned her eyes away, to the stack of today's newspapers:

THIRD ELDERLY WOMAN SLAIN
Police Seek Robber-Rapist

There was plenty of time for her to read the front-page story. Three murders of women over sixty in the past week, all in this area of the city, the first only three blocks from her apartment building. All the victims lived alone. All were beaten, raped, stabbed, and then robbed of televisions, computers, jewelry, money. The murderer seemed to know which solitary old women kept portable valuables.

Fear stabbed through the old woman's gut. All the victims were exactly like her! And it wasn't fiction. It was real.

Had there really been eyes on her when she opened the mailbox on her way out? Had she been followed? Or was the predator lying in wait?

What kind of mental illness made a man rape and murder old women? Old women didn't bother anybody. They didn't ask for trouble, like half dressed, flirty young girls.

Her head was spinning so that she hardly noticed when her cart came up to the checkout counter. "Hey, lady!" the woman at the cash register prodded. "I said $22.97."

She heard the woman behind her groan as she fumbled for her purse. Others before her had swiped credit cards, but she didn't have anything but the debit card her bank sent whether she asked for it or not. She never used it — had long since forgotten its assigned PIN number.

She counted out a ten-dollar bill, a five, and eight ones. Carefully, she returned the three pennies of change to the purse, snapped it firmly shut, and shoved it securely into her suit pocket, under her coat. Then she picked up her bag of groceries and trudged out into the night, her mind still a miasma of anger and fear.

It was those books — those vicious stories of sex and murder. True, she had written murder mysteries, but they had always begun discreetly after the crime was committed. If there had to be a description of the corpse, it was clinical, not sensational — and not disgusting like those Crime Scene television shows! The interest was whodunit, not how it was done.

And never — never once in all her thirty-seven novels and countless short stories — had she written about rape!

Oh, it wasn't fair, it just wasn't fair. Raping old women was unnatural. That's all people read these days, or watched on television: stories about unnatural acts. No wonder the world had gone mad!

She turned off the brightly lit avenue of stores, past office buildings and apartments. Toward the end of the block she walked beside the fenced-in schoolyard, deserted at this time of night.

A man and a woman stood at the bus stop, talking and laughing. The woman was young, pretty, wearing a suede jacket, plaid skirt, leather boots. Too well-dressed for this part of town — and she was white, the man with her black. Slumming,

She deserves whatever she gets, thought the old woman. I mind my own business, don't ask for trouble — and I could be raped and murdered. But there she is, asking for it, like the girl in that book who went looking for her no-good drug addict brother. At least she had the excuse of family!

Speeding her pace, she hurried past the couple, moving along briskly until her arthritic hip gave a twinge. It was still winter in her bones. As she turned into her street, she peered from side to side, hoping to see someone she knew, hoping not to see strangers lurking.

There were so many places to hide! And this neighborhood still had the old streetlights that made pools of light directly beneath them, leaving everything else in shadow. The change to new lights had stopped short when the city ran low on tax revenue three years ago. Side streets retained large areas of darkness.

The streets where old women live — what do they care about the safety of old women?

A cat squalled from a nearby roof, and a chill of fear went through the old woman. Warmer weather meant cats fighting and mating. It also made it more comfortable for muggers to lie in wait for their victims.

Most of the ground-floor apartments she passed were dark, windows broken, some patched with cardboard. No one wanted to live where it was easy for burglars to get in — so squatters moved in.

She was almost home when she heard a footstep behind her. Her heart thudded. She dared not turn to look, but cold sweat prickled over her skin. Her bag of groceries was heavy, but it wasn't much of a weapon. She inventoried its content in her mind as she climbed the steps to the foyer, almost ran to the stairs, and turned to make her stand.

Setting the bag on the stairs, she groped into its depths for the can of cling peaches. He wouldn't expect his intended victim to lie in wait for him with a blunt instrument —

The footsteps approached the building . . . stopped . . . went on. Stopped again or faded into the distance? She couldn't be sure. If he was going somewhere else, why did he pause here?

Listening for my footsteps, just as I listened for his!

She strained to hear if he was coming back. Nothing. There were eight apartments in the building. He might be standing down the street now, waiting for a light to tell him where an old woman lived alone, easy prey.

But this old woman was a mystery writer. She knew some tricks herself.

She picked up the bag of groceries, hoping the rustle could not be heard through the foyer in case he had crept back, and tiptoed up the stairs, walking along the side of the treads so they would not creak.

At her door she paused, listening intently. Nothing. Her keys jingled slightly — next time she would take only the door key. Live and learn. *Learn and live.*

Then she was inside, closing the door, throwing the bolt, sliding the chain into place.

She had left the desk lamp on. Deliberately, she did not turn on the overhead light. If the robber/rapist/murderer were watching her building, he wouldn't know where she was.

The kitchen was a tiny room off the living room. It had no windows, just an exhaust fan that didn't work most of the time. She put the groceries away, the heavy can of peaches last.

Back in the living room, her desk was an island of light. The typewriter sat unused, neatly covered. Her latest novel, almost completed, was stacked into a three-shelf organizer: original, copyright carbon, author's carbon. She hadn't written a word in over a month. Why bother? No one would publish it.

The last ribbon she had been able to get for the typewriter was stored in its foil pack in the bottom drawer, along with a pack of carbon paper. Soon she would not be able to work simply because she could not get her tools.

Her granddaughter had assured her when she visited at Christmas that if she could use a typewriter she could use a computer, but —

But nothing! She might be old, but she wasn't stupid. Tomorrow she would call her granddaughter and ask for advice on how to find the easiest-to-use computer: supposedly a basic machine cost no more than she had paid thirty years ago for that top-of-the-line electric typewriter.

If she scrimped a bit more, perhaps.

Or . . . how much would it cost to hire that bored housewife in #307 to copy her book onto disk? One day in the laundry room, the younger woman had waxed rhapsodic about the wonders of the Internet, saying it was much better than television.

Where there was a will there was a way. If the publishers wanted books typed on computers, she would give them books typed on computers!

But no one wanted her kind of books, skillfully-plotted murder mysteries. They wanted thrillers with lots of blood and no logic, appropriate to a world in which old women were beaten and raped and robbed —

The man who had followed her. Was he the murderer of those other old women? Or someone who had read about them in the paper and, seeing her, had for a moment considered emulating the headlines?

She had made it too hard for him. He should go after flirty young women looking for trouble. They were the ones who deserved it, the women of *Sordid Saturday* and *City Heat*.

She picked up the three-tiered desk organizer, and tipped its contents into the trash can. Then she uncovered the typewriter, rolled in an original and two carbons, and began to write about a rapist/murderer. She didn't start after his victim was discovered, but while she was still alive, young, pretty, flirtatious, wearing a suede jacket, plaid skirt, leather boots —

*****

The bus ride was long and boring, but tonight the young teacher had too much on her mind to resent the hour spent each direction. She held her briefcase on her lap, eager to read the papers inside.

Her talk with the black student had been stimulating, exciting, in spite of the fact that his reverence for the written word bordered on superstition. What a marvelous notion — that in the illiterate slave culture of his great-great-grandmother's time, her literacy should appear a form of magic!

She wondered if there was a thesis in there somewhere. Folklore. Word magic. Where did truth end and superstition begin?

The fresh, new ideas still glowed so brightly in her head when she got off the bus that she failed to notice the man lurking in the doorway of a closed store nearby, or that when she passed him, the heels of her boots ringing against the sidewalk, he sidled out and began to follow her.

It was almost eleven o'clock. Most of the windows were still lit in the apartments along this street, rented out to students. Music pulsed through the air.

But in this neighborhood, too, the street lights were the old-fashioned kind that didn't penetrate the shadows. No one was out on the street except the young teacher and the man following her. The slight sound his sneakers made was easily drowned by the clack-clack of the young woman's heels. He kept one streetlight behind her, so that as her shadow danced its elliptical pattern through the pools of light, his did not appear to partner it.

When she turned into the walk to her building, the man speeded his pace. She stopped in the shadows and set down her briefcase to unlock the door to the courtyard.

As she moved to keep her own shadow from

blocking the dim light falling on the keyhole, another shadow fell over it.

*****

UNIVERSITY GRADUATE STUDENT
RAPIST-MURDERER'S LATEST VICTIM

*****

A few months later, a new book appeared on the supermarket rack. *Night in the City*: rapist/murderer stalks young women who dare to walk alone.

"Ripped from today's headlines!" screamed the blurb on the cover.

The old woman, though, did not see her latest book in the supermarket where she used to shop. When she suddenly made a large advance, her granddaughter invited her to live with her, in a neighborhood where the streetlights were the new kind that obliterated shadows. Their building had a doorman, and television cameras in the elevators.

*****

In #307 of the old building, after her husband had gone to work and her son to school, a bored housewife poured herself another cup of coffee and sat down at her computer. She couldn't believe the drivel she'd keyboarded in for the old woman from #201 was actually on the bestseller list.

Well, if it was *that* easy —

Resisting the urge to check her email first, she opened her word processor and began to type:

> *The man hated single women. They refused to submit to the proper woman's life of caring for husband and children.*
> *He especially hated the successful ones, the ca-*

*reer women who lived in those fancy apartments
with doormen and TV cameras in the elevators. If
he only set his mind to it, he knew there had to be a
way to get around that security, reach those women
in their lairs —*

THE BEHOLDER

I do not make the rules of *magick natureel*. I do but abide by them.

The people of our small village by the sea come to me seeking magic, a charm to ward off illness, advice on when to plow or plant, or the best day to launch a new fishing boat. In all of those things, people are willing to abide by nature.

But in love they seek time and again to thwart nature, to give themselves beauty in another's eyes, or to force someone to love them.

It is in the pursuit of love that I have most often been mistaken, for charms and feelings forced by magic are not real. Over many years I have learned caution, but when I was young I thought everyone deserving of love. Perhaps it was a way of soothing mine own romantic feelings, for one thing a witch woman cannot do is make magic for her own use.

They say there is a man for every woman, no matter how unfavored she may be — one who will love her with his whole heart, let the world think what it will. Looking about any village in the land, you will see that sometimes even the poorest and ugliest have husbands who can see the true beauty in their hearts.

But only sometimes. Far more often they are miserable wretches, left to fend alone, or mistreated by loutish husbands. When I think of such misfortune, I cannot but recall the time when, still a young woman and new to my calling, I was asked not to make a charm, but to break one.

The young squire, son of the franklin, was of an age with me, but like the other girls of our village by the sea, I could only admire him from a distance. Of course he did not go to the local school, but had tutors until he was sent way first to the monks and then to university. When he came home, though, the village rejoiced. He was so beloved for his kind words and good deeds that people failed to mention what a handsome young man he had grown to be. Not that we young women failed to notice.

Jankyn provided venison when the harshest winter in memory froze the fishing fleet in the harbor. That same winter he gave the villagers firewood from the franklin's lands, and later sent his laborers to replace the mud-and-wattle houses that burned when people stoked the fires too high to ward off the bitter cold. Everyone spoke of his goodness and courtesy to all.

When a neighboring kingdom declared war, the young squire led a troop of local men, and returned a hero with a knighthood. That was when the franklin decided it was time for his son to marry . . . and that brought Jankyn to me.

When he appeared at my door, I thought he came seeking further charms against the disease stalking our community — the plague which always follows when times of deprivation have made people weak. His own father had been gravely ill, and when I saw Jankyn standing there my first fear was that the franklin had suffered a relapse.

But no, his father was improving daily — and for that very reason Jankyn had come to me with an extraordinary tale. It seemed that during his service in the army, our young squire had been wounded, temporarily blinded by an exploding cannon. A lady of the local gentry nursed him back to health. No surprise that he loved her before he ever saw her face.

"I fell in love with her gentle, capable hands," he told me, "and her voice, sweet and pure and intelligent."

"Intelligent? Her voice?" I asked, and he smiled at his own nonsense.

"What she said," he amended. "She sat and talked with me for hours when pain and the fear of blindness disturbed my rest. She is bright, charming . . . and I love her."

"Then what is the problem?" I asked. "Is she betrothed or married to another?"

"No. I told her that I loved her, and she told me . . . she is ugly. A man might love her as a sister, perhaps, but never as a man loves his wife."

"And is she right?" I asked.

He sighed. Then he replied, pain in his voice, "Her ugliness is far beyond ill-favor. I don't care . . . but my father will. When the bandages were to come off my eyes, Greta was not there. When my sight adjusted, I looked for her, but only the other women were present. They told me she could not bear to have me see her."

"But you could not be satisfied with that."

"Of course not! As soon as I had the strength to walk about the castle I went in search of her. She was with some gravely wounded soldiers who had just been brought in, nursing and comforting them. I followed her beautiful voice. She knelt praying by the side of a dying man, and I knew that God accepted his soul simply because Greta prayed that He would."

He paused, but I had nothing to say, so waited for him to continue his story. "She was facing away from me, kneeling. All I could see was her slender back as she bent over the man she had comforted and drew the blanket up over his face. When she rose, her back remained bent and crooked. She turned, and I saw her face. She had spoken truly: she is quite astonishingly ugly."

The words, spoken flatly, were wholly inadequate to express the pain I saw in the young squire's eyes.

"And?" I prompted.

"And I ran away!" he said angrily. "The very next moment I knew that I loved her no matter how she looked, but she had seen my unguarded reaction and refused to talk to me.

"My wounds had healed. I had to return to battle. God forgive me for that moment of weakness! I wrote to her from the field, begging her forgiveness, but received no answer."

"Did you return to the castle where you met her?"

"I wanted to, but as you know, my father was ill. As soon as the war was over I rushed home."

The young squire's return had been far greater tonic than any potion I could devise, but it was probably his brush with mortality that had put the idea of grandchildren so firmly I the old man's mind.

"Now your father wants you to choose a wife," I prompted, "but you are already in love with Greta."

"I can't think of anyone else, nor can I take an interest in the women my father introduces me to. I don't care what she looks like — Greta is the only woman I can imagine spending my life with."

"Then . . . what need have you of my spells?" I asked.

"I wish you to break a spell cast by another . . . the spell of Greta's ugliness."

"Ah," I said. "Then she was not born ugly."

"No. The other women told me the story. Greta's father and mother were childless, and finally went to a local wizard for a fertility spell. He cast the runes and found that they would have no sons, but their grandson would be a great leader of men. That pleased them, for if fate decreed a grandchild, fate must also decree a child. And so they left the wizard without commissioning the spell."

"I see. They insulted his power. And . . . did they compound their error by not paying him?"

"I'm afraid so," said the young squire. "Just over a year later their daughter was born, a beautiful baby girl they named Greta. But on the day they presented the child, just a few weeks old, to all their friends, the wizard appeared with a thunderbolt and a flash of lightning. 'I provided you with the joyous news of your future,' he told them, 'and in return you first insulted and then ignored me. I rescind that joyous future! This child will never give you grandchildren, for no man will ever willingly touch her!' and he waved his wand over the baby girl, who became instantly so hideous that her nurse screamed and turned away, and her own mother fainted."

"The poor child," I could not help but whisper, pitying the innocent victim of her parents' stupidity and a wizard's prickly pride.

"Greta does not think of herself as a poor child," said the young squire. "She has grown up good and kind. Her beauty is inside. But. . . ." He chewed his lip, trying to find words to explain.

"But your father will not accept beauty that cannot be seen, nor will the people of the village," I said flatly. "You seek to have the spell on her removed. But Squire, I am no wizard. I doubt I have the ability to persuade one to remove his spell."

"No," he replied. "That perhaps I could do, for even wizards have desires which a man might find a way to meet. But this wizard died some dozen years ago. He is not available to remove the spell. So . . . I have come to you."

I could offer the young squire no promises — I am a simple witch woman, no match for a wizard's power. The tiny hope I could provide came from the fact that the wizard was no longer available to counteract any spell I might devise. "But your first task," I told the young squire, "is to persuade Greta to come to me."

"That," he said, "I know how to do."

And indeed, not a fortnight later a ship from Greta's land sailed into our harbor, and from it embarked several ladies in gowns of plain design, along with one squat, limping figure dressed the same as the others except for the veil over her face, which allowed only a slit for her eyes.

I was privy to Jankyn's plan to bring Greta and the other lady nurses to our country. It was only half a lie that our village needed their help: the epidemic our soldiers had brought back was some fever our people had no resistance to. In the very old, the very young, and those weakened by the recent lean years, it often turned to pneumonia. Everywhere, people nursed friends and family members, falling with exhaustion themselves.

Greta and her ladies commandeered the guild hall as an infirmary. Within a day, everyone was blessing their help and kindness, and in particular praising the sweet voice and capable hands of the Lady Greta. Among strangers, she wore her veil at all times. Then, as she and I administered a fever-reducing potion to old Saul the baker, Saul's wife Marj and their daughters appeared with a cart laden with soup.

We had worked all night and half the day with nothing but a few mouthfuls of water. The soup smelled wonderful. "Sit ye down," Marj insisted. "We'll feed the patients. You ladies need nourishment yerseln," and she handed out bowls of hearty broth along with hunks of bread.

I sank gratefully to the floor, while Greta sat clumsily on a three-legged stool near the cloths we had hung to give the patients privacy. She turned away from old Saul and me as she lifted her veil.

"Lady Greta," I said, "you are among friends. You need not fear to show your face."

There was a long pause before she turned around, veil in place, holding the untouched soup and bread on her lap. "I must not disgust the patients while they are eating," she said softly. What struck me at that moment was the total absence of self-pity in her beautiful voice. There was only concern for the comfort of others.

"If anyone's disgusted," I told her, "such ungrateful louts deserve to miss a meal!"

I could see only her eyes, beautiful as Jankyn had said they were, and in them a tentative smile. Then, hesitantly, she unfastened her veil.

As the young squire had said, she was astonishingly ugly. Her nose turned up like a pig's snout, and crowded teeth emerged from her lower jaw to thrust upward like tusks. They distorted her mouth, pushing her chin forward aggressively.

The beauty of her eyes was hidden by heavy bone above and beneath them, so that when not framed by her veil they seemed to disappear, great hairy brows obscuring their luminescence. It was a face to frighten children . . . but we were no children in that room. All of us managed to contain our horror and pity in the face of Greta's courage.

"Eat up," I managed to say in quite natural tones. "Marj's soup wins at the autumn fair every year!"

Eating was a painfully slow process for Greta. Her distorted mouth could take only small bites of food if she did not want to risk it squirting out and running down her chin. Obviously, she had practiced long and hard to achieve grace at table, but nevertheless we all stared in horrified fascination.

Deliberately, I turned to start a conversation with Marj and her daughters. Usually they were reticent about talking to the witch woman, never sure when some casual comment might offend, or give me power over them. But their desire not to embarrass poor Greta produced a conversation long enough to allow Greta some nourishment.

I came away from that encounter determined to help Greta if it was humanly possible. The epidemic was nearly over, and she and her ladies would soon leave. I spent the night poring over my tomes, searching for a way to take off the hideous spell of that oversensitive wizard. If bad fortune had turned her sour, I would probably not have cared, but Greta deserved better than life had dealt her. Life isn't fair, but one of the few joys of magick is occasionally being able to do something about it.

Greta and her ladies were quartered, when they spared time from the infirmary, at the franklin's great house. The young squire escorted them to and from the village, and worked his own wiles on Greta at every opportunity. It was obvious that he loved her; little wonder that he was able to win her love despite her lifetime of defenses.

Still, she would not have him. Despondent, he came to me again the day before the ladies were to sail for home.

"Can you make me a love spell?" Jankyn asked.

"You don't need one," I told him. "Anyone can see that Greta loves you."

"Then a spell to bind her here! Please! She's the only woman I'll ever love. Why can't she see that?"

"Because she always thinks of others rather than herself," I told him. "What does your father say?"

The young squire hung his head. "He says . . . he loves Greta as a daughter already, but fears to have deformed grandchildren." Then he looked up at me. "Greta also fears her children will inherit her appearance. I've reminded her of the prophecy, that one of her children will become a great leader. Surely her true nature is what will be passed on to her children. Still, she will not budge."

"Bring her here," I told him. "I have been studying everything I can find about wizards' spells."

"Can you take the spell off?" Jankyn demanded.

"I don't know," I replied honestly. "Bring Greta here tonight, and I will tell you my conclusions, and the decisions you will have to make."

Magick is a complicated business. Oh, some is quite straightforward, knowing which poultices will staunch bleeding or stimulate a healing fever, but a great deal depends on the state of the human heart . . . both the hearts of the persons for whom the spell is done, and mine own.

I don't think I have ever sought to do magick with a purer heart than I did that evening. I had no power to lift the spell that crotchety wizard had put on Greta. Had he lived to see the strong and blessed woman she had become, he would surely have been shamed into removing it — probably for rich reward and undeserved gratitude. But he was dead, and the spell was permanent.

However, I found a countercharm, a spell upon a

spell as it were, but one that would require a hard decision from Jankyn and Greta.

When they arrived, I told them the good news first. "The spell is only on you, Lady Greta. Any children you have will be as beautiful as if no spell had ever been cast."

"That answers my father's only objection!" said Jankyn.

"It is still unfair to burden you with such an ugly wife," Greta protested.

"Do you love Jankyn?" I asked Greta.

It was not coyness that made her hesitate, but finally, "Yes," she admitted.

"Would you marry him if you could be beautiful for him?"

"Yes," she replied. "But a witch woman cannot remove the spell of a wizard." Obviously I was not the only one who had done research.

I brought forth my magic mirror. "I do not like what I see in the mirror," Greta objected. "I accept it, but I do not like it."

"Jankyn, stand behind her," I instructed. "Now both of you look at Lady Greta's reflection."

Jankyn put a hand on her shoulder to give her courage, and together they stared at the ugly, distorted visage reflected in the glass.

This was a simple illusion. A moment's concentration, and the face in the mirror changed. Gone were the tusks, the ugly growths of bone, the matted overgrown brows. The nose assumed a normal shape above a sweetly smiling mouth. Beautiful, serene eyes emerged from obscurity. "This is how Lady Greta would have looked without the wizard's spell."

Greta's chin trembled, and tears slid down her cheeks — sparkling crystal drops in the mirror, wet tracks on either side of a reddened nose in reality. But while Jankyn's eyes remained, entranced, on the image in the mirror, Greta's fixed on me. "Why do you torture us? You cannot make me look like this image."

"But I can."

At that, Jankyn gasped and turned to look at me as well. "How?" he asked. "What do I have to do? I'll pay you anything to end Greta's suffering!"

"Jankyn," Greta interrupted, "I do not suffer, except that I see you suffer."

"Lady Greta," I said, "if I could make you look as you did in the mirror just now, why would you want it?"

"So that I could be the wife that Jankyn deserves."

"And Jankyn — why would you want it?"

"So the world would see Greta as she truly is."

I sighed. "Unfortunately, her appearance is not an illusion. I have no way of changing her flesh and blood form."

"Then . . . what are you offering?" asked Jankyn.

"A charm, a spell, to cause Greta's . . . soul, her personality, to be seen instead of her flesh and bone."

"Another illusion," Greta said sadly. "I see no benefit to some temporary charm." She waved her hand at the mirror, which now gave back all her external ugliness.

"No, not temporary," I said. "I will tie my spell

into the strength of that spell the wizard cast on you. If it is ever lifted, then so will be the illusion I create. But then," I said with a smile and a shrug, "you won't need my spell anymore, will you?"

I had thought Greta didn't smile because she had little to smile about. Now I saw the hideous distortion of her face as she turned to Jankyn. But he did not misinterpret the grimace. "Do it!" he said. "I don't care what it costs!"

"Your favor," I told him. "Your protection in those times when I become a convenient scapegoat."

"That is nothing you would not have had anyway."

"Then you must make a choice."

"What choice?" Greta asked.

"A hard choice," I told them, "and a test of your love. There are some spells designed to test the character, and the only one I could find to restore your appearance, my lady, is one of those. There is no way I can make everyone see you as beautiful."

"Jankyn is the only one I care about," she replied.

"That may be your choice, but there is another. Each of you must choose, in your heart of hearts, who will see you as beautiful, and who will see you as ugly.

"Jankyn, Greta can be beautiful to you and ugly to everyone else. If you so choose, you will have the comfort of her loveliness, but she will continue to suffer as she does now: strangers will be repulsed by her, children will fear her, and even those who know and love her will pity her.

"The other option is that she will appear beautiful to everyone else . . . but you alone will face her ugliness. What you see before you now is what you will face all the days — and all the nights — of your lives together. Other men will envy you your beautiful wife, but you will never enjoy her beauty."

"Jankyn," Greta whispered, "I cannot do that to you. I don't care about the rest of the world — I'm used to their stares, their pity."

"No!" he insisted. "I love *you*, Greta. I don't care what you look like to me — but you must be free from stares and pity."

Had I been in Greta's place I would have found arguments to cast aside public ugliness. I would have told my lover that the heir to his father's estate must have a wife appropriate to his station. And had I been in Jankyn's I would have argued that the people already loved her, and had no need of a beautiful exterior to be persuaded of her worth.

I could not help but feel a stab of jealousy at their pure, unselfish love, and a grim satisfaction in knowing that these perfect lovers would spend that night in argument. "You must decide," I told them, "before sunrise tomorrow. As the sun rises, divide this potion and each drink off your half, holding your choice in your heart. From that moment on, things will be as you have chosen. But take heed: if you wish at cross-purposes, you will nullify the spell."

Jankyn took the potion with trembling hands, and tucked it carefully away. Hand in hand, he and Greta left my hut.

Despite my weariness from the hard work during the epidemic, and nights spent searching for a solution for Jankyn and Greta, curiosity had me up at dawn. I found the village abuzz even at that early hour: Greta was not leaving with the rest of the ladies!

So they must have come to some agreement. I was desperate to know which they had chosen — his comfort, or hers.

When the franklin's carriage arrived in the village square, Jankyn's father emerged to announce that his son and the Lady Greta were engaged to be married. The cheer from the assembled villagers warmed even my weary heart: no matter what Greta looked like to them, they had learned to love her. Then Jankyn emerged, somewhat shamefaced, and turned to hand Greta out.

She was as ugly as ever — either they had wished at cross-purposes or Jankyn had yielded to his own selfish interest.

But then, as Greta climbed the guildhall steps to stand beside Jankyn, I heard gasps of astonishment around me. "That's not Greta!" someone exclaimed.

"She's beautiful!" cried another.

And Marj the baker's wife broke out sobbing, "Love broke the spell! Ah, ain' she the most beautiful thing you e'er seen?"

It was my spell Greta wore — obviously I was the only person there immune to it. But why should Jankyn look ashamed if he had chosen Greta's comfort over his own . . . unless he was having second thoughts about the pleasures of his marriage bed?

But as love and joy poured from the crowd, I saw Jankyn's look change to utter joy. I felt a swell of pride in this man who had sacrificed his personal pleasure to end his bride's life of misery . . . and another stab of jealousy to know there was such a man in the world, and that he belonged to another.

But along with joy I saw puzzlement on the young squire's face. He stared from Greta to the crowd and back again, as if he could not believe his eyes or ears.

Before my uncharmed eyes, Greta blushed an ugly red and smiled her distorted grimace, but Jankyn beamed as if she were as smooth faced and sweet lipped as the harvest queen.

I worked my way through the crowd, both to congratulate the happy couple and to try to find out what in the name of all magick had happened. Jankyn called me forward to announce that I had broken the spell on Greta.

"No," I told him as the crowd broke up and we joined the franklin in ambling toward the tavern, "you two did it."

"You said it would work only one way," said Greta. "Why does everyone say I'm beautiful when we wished only for Jankyn to see me that way?"

"I didn't," said Jankyn. "*I* wished for everyone else to see you beautiful — but when I saw you this morning I cursed myself, thinking that in my secret heart I must have wished selfishly and condemned you to a life of ugliness."

Greta turned to me with a frown that on the visage I saw was thoroughly intimidating. "You said if we wished at cross-purposes, nothing would happen."

"No," I explained, "I said that it would nullify the spell, which has been my past experience. But in those cases, no matter the unselfish words they spoke, each party in his heart of hearts made his wish to his own advantage. This is the first time I have ever known both parties to such a spell to choose *un*selfishly."

I never told Jankyn and Greta that I alone continued to see the blushing bride as hideous, nor that I do so to this day. Over the long years, I'm told, she has evolved from a young woman's loveliness to an elegant maturity. I see a hunchbacked crone.

No matter, of course, except to me. I suppose I shall never know if my first thought was correct, and I cannot be fooled by my own spell . . . or whether that stab of jealousy I felt and still sometimes feel at the total love Greta found in Jankyn condemned me alone to witness her outward ugliness as a reminder of my inward imperfection.

Greta gave Jankyn three children, all perfect and beautiful, and they continue as happy as it is possible for mere mortals to be. Their son is a young man grown now, and has already gained favor with the king for his courage and wisdom — he is well on his way to fulfilling the prophecy that he will be a great leader. Their older daughter married an earl, and recently presented them with twin grandsons.

And I live out my days alone in my cottage on the cliff side, for all my magical knowledge a mere onlooker to their selfless love . . . a human condition which before Jankyn and Greta I did not believe possible. They live what I know in the abstract but have never experienced: beauty is seen by the heart, not the eyes, and unselfish love can work miracles.

But in my whole long lifetime, theirs is the only such miracle I have ever witnessed.

THE ROOSTER
UNDER THE TABLE

A FOLKTALE RETOLD
with Lois Wickstrom

Once upon a time, in a land of magic, there was a princess who didn't want to marry. She wanted to have adventures, or rule a kingdom like her father. She didn't like sitting around in pretty dresses, eating daintily with fancy silverware, and speaking in a soft, ladylike voice. And those were the only things a princess, or a queen, ever got to do.

Her father, the king, was an old-fashioned man. He wanted his daughter to marry. But he wasn't so old-fashioned that he would marry her to a man she didn't like. He issued a proclamation: "Any man who can win my daughter's consent to marry will earn half my kingdom now, and the rest when I die."

Soon young men lined up outside the castle for miles, all waiting to win the princess and half the kingdom. True to his generous nature, the king had hot food brought to the young men every day as they waited in line. And at night, he had warm blankets and pillows brought to them by his faithful servants. One after the other, the princess rejected each young prince when his turn came to ask her consent to marry.

After several months, the king became frustrated with all these freeloading princes who ate his food and slept in his blankets, and waited in line all day only to be rejected by his daughter. Feeding them was expensive. And they kept his servants so busy that they didn't have time to keep the castle clean.

So, the king issued a new proclamation. "Any man who can win my daughter's consent to marry will earn half my kingdom. But if he fails, he will forfeit his life."

When they heard this new announcement, most of the princes went home. Half a kingdom and a beautiful wife would be nice to have, but the chance wasn't worth having their heads chopped off.

The princess became disturbed at her father's new proclamation. She didn't want to marry, but she also didn't want to be responsible for young men having their heads chopped off.

So she took off her beautiful lace-trimmed princess dress, and put on the gardener's old muddy overalls. She stopped washing and combing her hair. She refused to take a bath. Then she squatted under the dining room table. When the young princes asked for her hand in marriage, she flapped her arms like rooster's wings and would only answer, "Aawk, Aawk."

She refused to eat anything except raw grains and bits of fruit that dropped to the floor when others ate. She became the opposite of a princess. No pretty clothes, no dainty eating, and no soft voice.

Soon word got out that the princess wasn't worth the risk of losing one's head. And the king only had to feed a prince or two each week, as they took their chances and lost. Soon the princes stopped coming altogether.

Now among the princes who had journeyed from afar was the youngest of seven sons. He was a true prince, but after his six older brothers had received their inheritance, all that was left to him was the clever rooster, Chanticleer. So he had come to court the princess in hopes of earning a kingdom of his own.

As soon as he arrived, however, he heard the news that the princess had stopped washing and combing her hair, and was living under the table, refusing to say anything but "Aawk, Aawk."

Chanticleer, the clever rooster, said, "It sounds as if she just wants to be a rooster under the table. That princess won't be marrying anyone, and you are a fool if you try to court her."

Out of money and out of luck, the young prince replied, "I must court her anyway. There are no princesses in need of rescuing from dragons or ogres, so this is my only opportunity to win a kingdom."

"But she will refuse you, and then you will just get your head cut off," said the clever rooster. "What good will that do anybody?"

"What good do I do anybody now?" asked the prince. "Without a kingdom to rule, a prince is nothing. I may as well court the princess and risk getting my head cut off."

"Wait, young sir!" said Chanticleer. "Let me go into the castle and see what the princess really wants. That may take a while, so if you want to eat in the meantime, you'd better get a job."

"A prince get a job?" exclaimed the young man in surprise.

"If a princess can be a rooster under the table, then a prince can earn his keep," said the clever rooster.

So the young prince took the only job in that kingdom available to a strong young man with no experience: helping to care for the pilgrims in the local hostelry for those who fell ill or were injured on their journey. At first he found the work hard, for he had never cared for other people in his life, but as the days passed and he saw the grateful looks on the faces of those he fed or gave water to, heard his name included in the prayers of those he lifted and cleaned after, he discovered that he liked helping others.

*****

Meanwhile, Chanticleer flew over the castle wall and found his way into the great hall where the princess now lived under the table. She was indeed a sad sight, all dirty and unkempt, and hunched over like an animal. When he approached her, she cried "Aawk! Aawk!" and shook her arms awkwardly at him as if indeed she were trying to be a rooster under the table.

So the clever rooster ran at the princess, crying "Aawk! Aawk!" and shaking his wings at her. The princess began to imitate his movements and his squawking, becoming even more like a rooster under the table.

When people eating at the table dropped raw grains or bits of fruit, the princess and the real rooster shared them. They became roosters together under the table.

The princess and the clever rooster lived like this for several weeks, with the princess learning to act more and more like a real rooster. The king saw that his daughter was happy, so he let her and the rooster continue living under the table.

*****

Back at the hostelry, the young prince was assigned to help the cook. The cook set him to sifting weevils out of the flour. "This is terrible!" said the prince. "Sick and injured people shouldn't have to eat bread made from flour infested with weevils!"

So he went to the clerk who did the purchasing for the hostelry, and offered to go with him to the miller on his next trip to buy flour. The prince had been trained in how to run a castle, so he knew how to bargain for the best flour at the best prices, and how to keep the miller from cheating, so they returned with clean, fresh flour with no weevils.

"I want you to come along with me on market day!" said the clerk. Soon all their patients were eating better and getting well faster. As he watched a knight healed of a broken leg walk out the door, the young prince felt as proud as if he were ruling his own kingdom.

*****

In the great hall of the castle that same day, somebody dropped a piece of toast under the table where the princess and the rooster were living. Chanticleer pounced on it and ate it.

The princess was shocked! "How can you eat toast, which has been cooked, if you are a rooster under the table?" she asked.

The clever rooster replied, "You've known me for months now. I am a rooster under the table, just like you. You can do anything you want to do, and still be a rooster under the table."

The princess stared at Chanticleer, realizing that a rooster had just talked to her. Seeing her consternation, the clever rooster flapped his wings and squawked, "Aawk! Aawk!" The princess saw that he could eat toast, and he could talk — and yet he was still a rooster under the table.

Several more weeks passed, and somebody dropped a comb under the table. Chanticleer saw the princess eyeing it, and fingering her matted hair. So he began preening his feathers, as he did every day. "Why don't you comb your hair?" he asked the princess. "You can preen your plumage and still be a rooster under the table." And he continued to smooth all his feathers into place.

The princess watched the clever rooster and thought about it. He did preen his beautiful red feathers every day, and yet he was still a rooster under the table. So she picked up the comb and began to work the knots out of her hair.

*****

Meanwhile, the young prince was so successful at bargaining for supplies for the hostelry that the clerk in charge asked him to come along on a journey to the stone quarry, to get stone to repair the walls of the hostelry.

The journey was not long, but the return was hard, carrying the heavy slabs of stone on flatbed wagons. Therefore many men went together, among them the master mason in charge of repairs to the royal castle. He was so impressed with the bargaining abilities of the young prince that at the end of the journey he asked him to come to the castle the next day, as he believed this young man would make an excellent addition to the castle staff.

While the young prince was gone, Chanticleer noticed that the princess was more and more uncomfortable, scratching at her dirty skin. So one bright sunny afternoon he flew to the top of the courtyard fountain and proceeded to splash and bathe himself in the shallow dish there.

The princess followed the clever rooster out into the sunshine, squinting because she had not been outside in months. She stretched her body, which ached from squatting under the table and sleeping on the hard stone floor all that time, and rubbed her back as she said, "How can you go out in the sunshine and bathe in the fountain and still be a rooster under the table?"

Chanticleer flapped down to the paving stones, shook the drops of water from his feathers, flapped his wings, and squawked, "Aawk! Aawk!" Then he added, "You can do anything you want, and still be a rooster under the table."

"Anything?" asked the princess. "Can I really do anything I want, and still be a rooster under the table?"

"Of course," said the rooster, flapping his wings. "Anything you want."

And now that she understood, the princess, in this land of magic, realized that the magic was within herself. First she took a bath, and then she dressed in neither the muddy overalls she had worn for months nor one of the delicate lace dresses she despised, but in a plain loose dress that allowed her to move as she pleased. It didn't bother her in the least that people might take her for a servant — at last she was comfortable in her body, and she went in search of her father to become comfortable in her mind.

In her search for the king, the princess passed through the courtyard of the castle where workmen were unloading slabs of stone to repair a tower. There she saw the clever rooster who had spent the past months under the table with her, perched on the wagon seat, watching as a very handsome young man discussed something with the master carpenter and the lord chamberlain.

The young man was not only handsome. Unlike all the young princes who had come courting her, his face was kind as well, and his hands were calloused from work. *That is the kind of man I want to marry*, thought the princess. *I want a partner to rule the kingdom with me, not someone who only knows how to tell other people what to do.*

And then she remembered, *I can do anything I want, and still be a rooster under the table.* So she continued in her search for her father.

When the king saw his daughter, clean and neatly dressed, out from under the table and walking like a normal person, he was so overjoyed that at that moment he would have granted her anything. But the princess said to him, "Father, I have something important to tell you. The clever rooster Chanticleer has taught me that I can do anything I want, and still be a rooster under the table."

"And what do you want to do, my daughter?" asked the king.

"I want to choose my own husband. I want him to agree that he will not become king over me, but that he and I will share the kingdom together and rule jointly."

"I agree to that," said the king, "but where will you find a prince who will agree to such terms?"

"I will search until I find him," the princess replied. "But right now I must go and find the clever rooster who taught me that I can do anything I want, and still be a rooster under the table. Will you reward him, Father, with whatever he asks?"

"He's a rooster," said the king. "What could a rooster ask that I would be reluctant to grant — especially when he has given my daughter back to me? Yes, I will grant him anything he asks."

Meanwhile, the prince was eagerly telling Chanticleer what he had been doing all these weeks. "I was wrong when I said that without a kingdom to rule a prince is nothing. Helping the sick and injured to get well made me feel better than having noble blood ever did. Keeping good people from being cheated is more important than sitting on a throne — and there are far more opportunities for that than for killing dragons."

Just then the princess entered the courtyard from one direction and the master mason with the lord chamberlain of the castle from the other.

"This is the young man I was telling you about," said the master mason. "He has been in our kingdom only a few months, and he has done nothing but good. First he helped the sick and injured at the hostelry. Then he taught the clerk there how to bargain for the best food and not be cheated. Finally he went with us to the quarry, where he not only showed himself able to choose the best slabs of stone and not allow us to be cheated, but worked willingly with the laborers to load the stone and bring it back with us. I think you should hire him for the castle staff."

Hearing this, the princess thought, I was right. This is definitely the kind of man I want to marry. I wonder if I can persuade my father.

So the princess went out into the courtyard to meet the prince. As before, he took her for one of the servants, but he thought, *She is quite beautiful and seems very nice,* so he accepted the job the lord chamberlain offered him as purchasing agent, and began to court the princess.

Chanticleer, the clever rooster, cocked his head to one side and decided that perhaps it was best not to tell the prince that he was courting the princess, or the princess that the man she showed such interest in was a prince.

The princess continued to dress in her plain clothes, and spent many hours with the prince, learning all the things he knew about how to run a castle in preparation for the day when she would rule the kingdom. The prince was happy to teach her, delighted to find a woman who was interested in his concerns and yet had a mind of her own.

He heard from the gossip in the castle that the princess had stopped being a rooster under the table, and was acting like a normal young woman again, but he no longer cared. He had found someone he liked better than any princess he had ever met.

The feeling was mutual, and both the prince and the princess privately confided their feelings to Chanticleer. Every once in a while, too, the princess would remind Chanticleer that her father the king had promised to reward him with anything he asked, but the clever rooster only replied, "I will wait for the day when I need a special favor from the king."

Time passed, the prince performed exceptionally as the castle's purchasing agent, and on the day when the king gave out awards for exceptional service he learned that he was to receive a small parcel of land and a portion of gold. He took the opportunity to propose marriage to the princess, who he still thought was a servant like himself.

"I am willing to marry you," she told him, "but you know that as residents of the castle we must have the king's permission."

"I will ask him at the ceremony tomorrow," the prince replied.

The next day all the castle servants gathered in the great hall where the princess had spent so many weeks as a rooster under the table, but the only rooster under the table that day was Chanticleer.

The clever rooster stayed out of sight, watching to see what would happen. The princess was dressed as usual, in the neat plain clothes she had adopted when she had learned she could be anything she wanted to be. She looked like any of the serving women except that she was especially beautiful that day in her happiness at being in love and knowing that the man she loved, loved her in return.

The king proceeded to hand out the awards, and when it came the turn of his purchasing agent, the young prince came forward to accept the bag of gold coins and the deed to his parcel of land. Then he spoke: "Sire, I would ask another boon of you."

"And what might that be?" the king asked, a bit suspiciously.

"I ask permission to marry."

The king cheered up immediately, pleased at the sign that the bright young man would settle down. "Granted," he said. "Who is the lucky bride?"

At that, the prince held out his hand, and the princess came to his side and took it, looking adoringly into his eyes.

The king's blood pressure rose so swiftly that his face turned purple. He sputtered. "How *dare* you?!" he demanded. "You are a servant! How dare you presume upon my kindness to court the king's own daughter?!"

And then he called his guards. "Throw him in the dungeon!" he ordered, and the prince was dragged off despite the pleadings of the princess.

"Father — you promised I could choose my own husband," the princess protested. "This is the man I have chosen."

"I told you, you could choose any *prince* you wanted," the king reminded her. "You may set your requirements, daughter, but you must also accede to mine."

The princess stood her ground. "I will go back to being a rooster under the table, Father."

"Go ahead," the king replied. "At least there you will not be destroying the royal line."

So the princess crawled back under the table with Chanticleer. As the great hall emptied in near silence, she railed at the clever rooster, "You told me I could be anything I wanted to and still be a rooster under the table. But you were wrong. I can be a rooster under the table, but I can't marry the man I love."

"Yes you can," said Chanticleer, "if the king is a man of his word as I think he is. Take me to your father, and let us see if we can work this out."

The princess stared at the clever rooster and remembered, "The promise he owes you. You are willing to use it to help me?"

"I can do anything I want, too," Chanticleer replied. "And I want to make both you and the man you love happy."

So the princess took the rooster with her and went to her father's chamber.

"Have you come to apologize?" the king asked her.

"No, Father," replied the princess. "I have come to remind you of your promise to grant Chanticleer here anything he asks of you."

The king sighed, and spoke to the clever rooster. "Yes, I do owe you, for this is the second time you have gotten my daughter out from under that table. What would you like? A golden perch? A marble chicken coop with ten beautiful hens to be your harem? Tell me, and it's yours."

"Anything I ask?" asked Chanticleer.

"That was my promise," the king replied.

"Then I ask that you permit the marriage between your daughter and the man she loves."

"No," said the king. "He is a commoner and a servant. He cannot marry a princess."

"He can be a prince if you say the word," replied Chanticleer. "He can do whatever he wants, just as your daughter can do whatever *she* wants."

The king looked at his daughter. "Do you really want to be a rooster under the table again, squatting there all dirty and going 'Aawk, aawk' at everyone who tries to talk to you?"

"No," replied the princess. "I want to marry the man I love. If he can't be a prince, then I will be a commoner. Keep your promise to Chanticleer: permit the marriage, and my husband and I will go away and earn our living in another kingdom."

Then she smiled at Chanticleer and said, "You see? I have learned what you taught me. I really can do anything I want and still be a rooster under the table."

"I could permit the marriage," said the king, "and then immediately after the ceremony have the groom's head cut off."

"And I," replied the princess, "could then end my days as a grieving widow, never marrying anyone, and leaving your kingdom with no heir, ever."

The king sighed, knowing he was defeated now that his daughter truly understood that she could do whatever she wanted, one way or another. "Very well, my stubborn rooster under the table," he replied, "you may marry the man you love, if he will agree to your terms."

The prince was only too happy to agree, for he had already discovered how much fun it was to run a castle together — so why not a kingdom?

There was a magnificent wedding, and all the people cheered to see their princess married to a kind and clever man. The prince never did tell anyone that he was a prince, as it no longer mattered — everyone in the kingdom learned the story and the lesson, "You can do anything you want, and still be a rooster under the table."

And so they all became roosters together under the table, and lived happily ever after.

CHANGE OF COMMAND

The meeting should have been under way five minutes ago.

It's not like Edgar Wolfe to be late, thought Lyria Melladin just as the lights went out, to the rumbling accompaniment of the emergency door slamming.

At the stomach-sinking lurch of zero-gee, everyone in the small room grabbed at their chairs. "Just hang on," said Lyria into the darkness. "Emergency lighting will be on in a moment."

But it wasn't. Utter blackness continued, the only light the tricks their eyes played, creating patterns on the retina.

The terminal before Lyria should have been lit, but it wasn't. The hiss of the ventilators had stopped. There was no sound but six people's breathing.

With that many people in such a small room, the oxygen supply would soon be depleted. Wrapping her legs around her chair, Lyria said, "I'll see if I can raise anyone."

She knew her terminal blindfolded — a good

thing at this moment. Playing over the power switches, she expected the screen to glow to life. Nothing happened. She told herself the choking sensation was imagination; not enough time had passed for the air to be running out . . . or had it?

"Mr. Benrum," she said to the Vergian navigator, "how much time has passed since the power failure?"

"2.18 minutes."

"Ms. Welton, how much time do we have?"

"Eight minutes of consciousness, maybe. A few more minutes before brain damage . . . or death."

Lyria felt odd, unable to react to the thought. She went on automatically, "We are cut off. If the entire ship is not dead, we have eight minutes to attract attention." *Perhaps I'm going to die, too.*

"This room is soundproof and thought-shielded," said Welton.

"The door?" Benrum suggested.

"If we could bang on it," said Welton, "the vibration might carry. In fact, if we can pound on anything —"

Vron, the Arcadian chief accountant, said, "I can maneuver in free fall. Stay near the floor, lest we fall if gravity returns."

Before they could move, however, emergency lighting came on. MacGregor, the second vicechairman, gave such a start that he floated up from his chair, arms and legs flailing grotesquely. In a fluid motion, Vron rose beside him, captured him, and reseated him, saying, "Hold on. They'll have gravity back on at any moment."

The hiss of ventilators began first — then suddenly there was "up" and "down" again, and the world returned to normal. The door slid open to admit Edgar Wolfe, who demanded, "Are you all right? I've never seen a failure like that. Everything was out — even the computer!"

"The whole ship?!" asked Welton.

"No — just the board room. When I couldn't get in, or raise you, I started investigating."

MacGregor was sweating now, reacting after the fact. "A good thing," he said shakily. "You saved our lives."

"Lyria," said Welton, "I'll get on it right away. I can't imagine what could have caused such a failure."

"Engineering's working on it," said Wolfe.

"Then wait please, Jane," said Lyria. "Our meeting will be brief, and then it will be . . . all over."

The meeting had only one order of business: the final report on the death of Captain William Reading. Until the Board appointed a new Captain, who would bring with him his own Secretary, it was still Lyria's job to verify what went into the log.

No one sat in the Captain's chair. Ranged around the table were Vron, Chief Accountant and First Vice-Chairman; Benrum, the Vergian Chief Navigator; and the humans who made up most of the officers as their species made up most of the crew: Ian MacGregor, looking more like a grizzled spacer than Second Vice-chairman; Edgar Wolfe, young, energetic, Vice-Chairman in charge of Sales and one of the most successful salesmen the Corporation had; Ship's Engineer Jane Welton; and Katrina Sharf, Purchasing Agent.

Benrum presented a sheaf of printouts. "Captain Reading was a capable navigator," he said gravely, his kewpie doll features almost unrecognizable without his usual sunny smile. Vergians were the friendliest, most likable race of intelligent beings known to humans. Their natural buoyancy and love of life made them popular on Corporation starships.

Lyria had never seen Benrum so serious. The usual vivid blue of his skin was gray with sorrow as he said, "I have checked and rechecked the orbit Captain Reading calculated for his shuttle — it could not have resulted in that crash."

Welton reported, "Engineering studied everything that was left of the shuttle. The malfunction must have been in a part that was completely destroyed in the accident."

"You conclude that it was an accident?"

"There was no sign of sabotage. Every molecule of substance in the shuttle is accounted for."

"Is everyone agreed that it was an accident, then?" asked Vron.

Lyria wondered why he stressed that. The evidence had been studied yesterday, after computer enhancement had failed to decipher the flight recording. Today's meeting was a mere formality. "Do you have new information to offer, Mr. Vron?" she asked.

The Arcadian's great yellow eyes studied her dispassionately. "No, I have nothing to add."

Vron spoke Standard fluently, but it was necessary to listen to him carefully, as his voice was designed for song, not speech. His race were telepaths, for whom sound was a medium for abstract art.

When Vron spoke, he sometimes allowed melodic considerations to outweigh vocal inflection.

Lyria was glad the Arcadian did not wish to lengthen the discussion. Surprisingly, neither did MacGregor. He usually had some trivial matter to bring up — mostly, Lyria thought, because he would otherwise have nothing to say. Today, though, everyone wanted the painful job done quickly. Probably they also wanted to get out of the board room until Engineering could verify its safety.

They filed out silently. Everyone had offered condolences to Lyria earlier, at the memorial service. This final meeting was an embarrassment as far as the Captain's Secretary was concerned. They would all be at the next ship's board meeting. Lyria would not.

Outside the board room, a team from Engineering had torn a panel from the wall. Jane Welton joined them, saying to a rather pretty young woman, "Hardin, what are you doing here? You're confined to quarters."

"It's an emergency," the woman replied.

"What did she do?" Ed Wolfe asked.

"Hacked her way past the codes into records she's not cleared for," Welton told him.

"It was only to reach the ship's library," Hardin protested. "What do you care what I read in my leisure time?"

Welton gave Hardin a warning glare and continued, "During the last emergency, we had to page the whole ship for her. She's a brilliant engineer, but a real discipline problem."

The young woman in question looked annoyed,

but did not miss the opportunity to flash Wolfe a smile. *Two of a kind,* Lyria thought, although Ed Wolfe seemed to be overcoming his youthful indiscretions and settling into responsibility. Bill had had high hopes for him.

She hurried away from the scene, avoiding a public display of her feelings. The "last emergency" Welton had mentioned was Bill's death.

Ian MacGregor was standing hesitantly in the corridor, looking toward the scene in front of the board room. He still looked pale. "Are you all right, Ian?" Lyria asked.

"Oh, yes — of course," he replied brusquely, and turned down another corridor toward the flight deck.

Back in her quarters, Lyria set about packing, another way of postponing having to think. Finally, however, she could put it off no longer. She had to decide what to do now that Bill was dead. For the past five years, neither of them had thought of a future without the other.

She sat quietly staring at the small pile of objects that summed up her life: her contract, voided by Bill's death; her identification card; her bank card and credit stamp; her stock certificates. That was it, the story of a lifetime.

No . . . one more thing. Slowly, she removed the stargem ring from her left hand, placing it on the pile. Now that Bill was gone, it no longer symbolized commitment; it was just another asset.

Numbly, she spoke into the computer. "Request value estimate."

"1038 CR ± 98."

She could live for a year on that. With her abilities, she would have a new position well before a year was up. She was certain, in fact, that the Corporation would give her a job aboard another starship. A good Secretary never lacked work, and she had been a Ship's Secretary. Some other executive officer would certainly want someone with her experience.

The door buzzed. "Come in," she said mechanically.

When the door opened, and she heard no footstep before the sound of it sliding shut again, she looked toward the outer cabin and saw Vron standing there. He moved so quietly because Arcadians could not wear shoes over their clawlike feet.

"Yes, Mr. Vron?" she asked politely. The chief accountant would not intrude on her without a purpose; he was the most private person on board.

"Ms. Melladin." Lyria concentrated on his melodious tone, seeking something on which to focus her mind. He continued, "I have received a message from the Board. They have placed me in command of this ship."

Lyria nodded. "An obvious decision; you were second-in-command. Congratulations."

The Arcadian's yellow eyes blinked. "The Corporation has never before given a nonhuman command. I did not expect it."

"Oh, you'll manage," she said casually, wishing he would leave so she could return to her state of numbness.

"No, I do not think so."

Words and inflection matched in flatness. Lyria stared at the Arcadian, but there was nothing to be told from his face. Except for those which opened and shut eyes and mouth, there seemed to be no muscles in it. His head, shaped much like a human's, was covered with the same velvet fur as the rest of him. Only the fur saved him from appearing reptilian. His large yellow eyes had pupils that opened and shut like a cat's, closing to an unreadable slit in bright light. Not that they were readable now, even though they were open almost to circles in the subdued light of Lyria's quarters.

Below the eyes, Vron's face was a flat ovoid: no nose, no lips, although the slitted mouth could form words. It could not smile or sneer, though. Lyria had heard that telepaths like the Arcadians had no need of facial expressions.

"You . . . don't think you will succeed as Captain?" she asked in surprise.

"Not without help," he replied. "Please, Ms. Melladin, may I consult with you?"

Curiosity — the first feeling to penetrate the lid she had capped over her grief — made her say, "Yes, of course. Please come in. Sit down . . . Captain."

Vron took her desk chair, turned it and sat straddling it, facing her, his arms resting on the back. It was the only way an Arcadian could sit comfortably in a contour chair designed for humans. Otherwise, his wings got in the way.

They were not bird or bat wings, but membranes like those of the flying fox, stretching from the outer edge of either hand in great folds of skin, down the arms, the sides of the body, legs, and feet. In the confines of a starship they were nonfunctional and immensely inconvenient — the reason, no doubt, that

Lyria had never heard of another Arcadian working in such an environment.

"Ms. Melladin," said Vron, "I know you plan to leave the *Venture*. Have you another position waiting?"

"No, but I'll find one easily enough."

"Would you consider remaining aboard, as my Secretary?"

"I don't think that would work out," she said, not knowing why she refused so automatically until Vron replied.

"Then you do expect me to fail."

She looked into the unreadable face. "I had not truly considered it."

"But you know how the Board of Directors thinks. When I received my notice, I had to stop and consider why the Board chose me over the available human officers. You, a human, perceive it without having to reason it out."

"And how do you think the Board reached its decision?" she asked, curious again.

"There are two human officers who could have been promoted over me. MacGregor was third-in-command, but he is nearing retirement. He has years of experience, yet has never risen beyond third on any ship. He has already realized his full potential. Wolfe, on the other hand, has great potential, but is too young to be given his own ship.

"My executive ability has never been tested, but I am a reliable accountant. The Board undoubtedly expects me to maintain business until Wolfe matures enough for command. If I fail soon, MacGregor can take over temporarily. If I simply do not succeed very well, the Board will phase me out in a year or two, when Wolfe is ready."

"And what if you should succeed?" asked Lyria.

"You admit that possibility?"

"I didn't think you understood human thought processes so well, Vron. You just might succeed. What do you think the Board would do then?"

"They have already set a precedent with my promotion. If the *Venture* turns a profit, I don't think the Board Members will care who is in command."

Lyria studied him. "Do you want the job?"

"No."

"Then . . . ?"

"I do not wish to be phased out. If I refuse the promotion . . . you know the Board's opinion of such an attitude."

"Yes. They would find a way to get rid of you."

"So I must succeed at command . . . or leave the *Venture*. I do not wish to leave."

Lyria wondered why. Life among humans deprived the Arcadian both mentally and physically. A telepath had to keep constant blocks against the mental static of non-telepaths, while a winged man

"Aren't you very uncomfortable on board a starship?"

"Uncomfortable? Ah, you mean being unable to fly. It is inconvenient, but acceptable. I exercise regularly . . . and I have learned not to go about knocking things over. I have no intention of leaving the *Venture* if I can avoid it. Ms. Melladin . . . why this concern?"

"Curiosity," she explained. "I suppose it is also curiosity that prompts me to agree to remain as

Ship's Secretary."

Vron's face showed nothing, but something in his musical voice suggested relief. "Thank you. Please write yourself a generous contract. I shall depend heavily on your expertise. You should be suitably compensated."

"So that I won't decide to work against you?" Such was the power of the Ship's Secretary — and the reason that a new Captain always brought his own trusted Secretary with him.

"Under Captain Reading," said Vron, "the *Venture* has seen little infighting. Your reputation for honesty and discretion matches Bill's. I assume that if you could not accept without reservation, you would tell me so."

She noticed his use of Bill's first name. The Arcadian was always studiously formal. Was there a friendship there she had not known of?

"You're right," she said. "I would refuse."

"Then I shall rely on you. You were most efficient when the power failed in the board room today. Your calm command of the situation prevented panic."

"Thank you . . . but I wasn't really calm. I didn't care that much if I died."

"I hope you will once more recognize the value of your life, Ms. Melladin."

"Value," she said sardonically. "Yes, I can be of value to you, to the Corporation. For the time being, perhaps that will be enough."

"I did not mean monetary value," said Vron.

"I know you didn't. I'm sorry. I haven't been thinking straight since Bill's death. Work should enable me to get back to normal." She thought a moment. "Normally, I would have ordered a scan of the board room after today's incident, before the Engineering crew were allowed in."

"A scan of the interior? Except for the terminal operator, no one in the room could have caused the power to be shut off . . . and you did not cause it, did you?"

"No . . . but I want to find out what did."

"Order the scan, then," said Vron, "and let me know if you find anything unusual."

*****

The board room looked as it had when they left it. As the furniture was immovable, Lyria could not tell if it had been cleaned until she ducked to see the fingerprints across the table's shiny surface. Good. She was not too late to find any evidence the room had to offer.

Sitting at the terminal, Lyria watched the information play across the screen. Nothing on the ceiling. Oil, sweat, soap, lotions, normal and easily identified substances on the table, chairs, and lower walls. The floor yielded a few more items: a staple, a hairpin, several threads, innumerable hairs, a stylus . . . and a capsule.

A capsule?

"Identify and scan for fingerprints," Lyria directed.

It was an oxygen capsule . . . bearing Ian MacGregor's fingerprints.

She remembered MacGregor's startled thrashing when the lights returned. Caught in the act of taking the capsule? Why did he have one? Had he expected the power failure?

Lyria called up MacGregor's medical records. There it was: emphysema from a compression failure fourteen years ago, not severe enough for a medical pension or to require treatment other than occasional oxygen. Presumably he would always carry capsules, and today fright must have made him feel the same choking sensation she had — especially with his memories of a compression failure.

But the lights had definitely startled him. Guilt? Perhaps, for the capsule would give him —

"How long could a seventy-five-kilo human male survive on such a capsule with no other source of oxygen?" she asked the computer.

"Thirty to thirty-eight minutes," came the toneless reply.

So he had nervously dropped the capsule, probably hoping no one would notice that he could have had extra time had rescue been delayed.

At that moment, Lyria Melladin wanted more than anything to believe she understood exactly what had happened. The power failure was an accident, just as Bill's death was an accident. MacGregor's reactions were due to bad memories.

But she could not let it go at that. Suppose Bill had been murdered?

Benrum had said he checked the orbit Captain Reading calculated. At the meeting, Lyria's mind had not been working. Now it was. Was the orbit he calculated the one programmed into the shuttle's console?

She spoke the proper codes to release the information. Her fingers played over the console, seeking the clues to whether the program had been falsified. It had been, very skillfully. Who could do such a thing? Who had the skill? She had. Vron had. Ian MacGregor definitely did not.

Edgar Wolfe. The only ship's executive who had not been in the board room also had the skill to substitute another shuttle orbit for the one Bill had calculated.

Lyria put the two orbits side by side on the screen. The false one ran so close to the correct one until the last few seconds that the man in the shuttle would have discovered his danger too late for manual override.

Oh, Bill!

Edgar Wolfe had the knowledge, and the motive. With Bill out of the way, he stood a good chance of promotion to Captain. But why today's incident? To get rid of the other candidates? Again her fingers flew, seeking beneath the carefully coded programming to find out how all power to this one room had failed — including power to the computer, whose source was independent of the life-support systems.

The Engineering crew had found a short circuit where the two systems came together. Now Lyria found that it had been programmed to short out.

Sorrow and anger vying for supremacy, she rose to seek out Vron, to tell him what Wolfe had done. In the corridor, she almost collided with Jenny Hardin. "Sorry," she said brusquely, ignoring Hardin's startled look as she hurried past.

Vron's cabin door opened to her palm, but Vron wasn't there. She had never been in the Arcadian's quarters before. They were starkly simple — nothing for wings to knock over or get caught on. The only personal touch was a startling one: the entire back wall was one huge mirror. Then she realized, at least partially, the kind of claustrophobia a man born to fly must feel within the confines of a starship.

As she entered the main area, an angry buzzing arose from off to her right. Startled, she turned to see a glass case full of swarming, insectlike creatures. Definitely not the kind of pets she would want!

Stepping to the desk, she was about to use the intercom to locate Vron when her eye fell on a pile of printouts. The top sheet showed the same two orbits she had gotten from the computer only minutes before. She leafed through them: Vron had recorded her investigation! Not only that; he had made permanent copies.

Why? Did he distrust her?

Or . . . was Vron the murderer? He, after all, had become Captain through Bill's death. He had the ability to program the computer to kill. Had he asked for her help to divert suspicion?

Had Vron expected to be the only survivor of the power failure? What was the Arcadian rate of oxygen consumption? She was about to ask the computer when the door opened and Vron swept in. "Lyria! I got a call that you were injured, and then when I got there —"

"I'll bet!" she said angrily. "Don't bother to lie, Vron. What've you been doing — planting more evidence against Ian MacGregor or Edgar Wolfe? You don't have to kill anyone else — you've got the Captaincy."

"What are you saying?"

"Are you going to kill me? That would be pretty hard to explain, wouldn't it? Right here in your own cabin?"

"Why don't you sit down and tell me what makes you think I would want to kill you?"

For the first time, Lyria found herself able to read the Arcadian's tone of voice: enforced calm over bewildered hurt. It stopped her panicked tirade, and she began to think more calmly — but remained on her feet.

"You were spying on me." She gestured at the printouts. "You know I've found out Bill was murdered. You anticipated that someone would find it out, so you arranged to divert suspicion with this morning's power failure. Did you arrange for Wolfe to be late?"

"He was delayed by Ms. Hardin, from Engineering."

"And you expected him to arrive too late to save the rest of us?"

"Ms. Melladin . . . had you died, I would have died also. In fact, my rate of oxygen consumption is higher than yours."

"But you could have taken MacGregor's oxygen capsule. Is that what was happening when the lights came on? Did you mean to take it from him?"

"How would I have known that he had such a capsule?"

"It's in his medical records. Besides — you're a telepath."

"Mr. Benrum is a telepath. In an emergency, he would drop his shields. He would be obligated to report any such act on my part."

"Oh. I suppose that's right. Um. Maybe you can fool another telepath, though. Or else you had Wolfe delayed only long enough to turn suspicion against him. He does have the computer knowledge —"

"Ms. Melladin . . . are you ready to hear the truth now?"

"I'm ready to hear your side of the story."

"I did not kill Captain Reading. Until you discovered the evidence, I did not know he had been murdered. I activated my console simply to locate you, and your program came up on my screen. I soon realized what you had found — and made permanent copies that cannot be erased through the ship's system."

"You keyed for me and got my program? That shouldn't happen."

"The privacy safeties have obviously been tampered with."

Lyria shook her head. "There was no warning that someone was logging in, either. Changing the security programming is a long, delicate job. Someone planned this murder very carefully."

"That someone has now jammed the computer circuits," said Vron. "Forgive me — I assumed that you were emotionally upset, and forgot to set privacy. I thought you jammed the circuits after discovering that I was recording your program. So I started for the board room — but Ms. Hardin called to say you had left there, and been injured."

"Hardin? I don't understand. She saw me leave the board room. Now why — ?"

"She sent me in a different direction so that we would not meet. That gave her time to destroy the evidence before you could show me. When I didn't find you, I went to the board room and found it sealed for cleaning."

Lyria said, "I set it to refuse all such orders before I left. We are dealing with someone with a high level of computer skill."

"If the motive were promotion," said Vron, "Wolfe, MacGregor, and I theoretically had such motive. Only Wolfe or I might be able to override the computer's defaults. Where does Jennifer Hardin fit in?"

"I hardly know her," said Lyria. "She's an engineer. Her programming skills are good enough to hack into the restricted areas of the ship's library. Let's check her record."

"The console is jammed," Vron reminded her.

"Its software is. Let's try a hardware solution. Where are your tools?"

Vron had his hand on a drawer handle when the door slid open and Edgar Wolfe said, "Hold it right there!"

Lyria turned. Wolfe, MacGregor, and Hardin all held hand weapons trained on Vron and Lyria.

"We know what you've done," said MacGregor, his voice shaking. "You two killed Captain Reading, and today you tried to kill me, and make it look like Ed did it."

Lyria suddenly knew where Hardin fit in. "It wasn't your idea, was it, Ian?" she said gently.

"What do you mean? It was your idea. You and that BEM kill off the Captain, then me, stick Ed here with the murder charge, and take over the ship!"

"Vron and I would have died in the board room

today," said Lyria. "We have to breathe, too."

MacGregor groped for an answer. "You know about my lung problem. They've used it as an excuse not to promote me for the past five years. I'd have gone first. If Ed hadn't been delayed, you would have been unconscious by the time we were rescued — but I'd have been dead."

"This is a very strange story," said Vron. "Mr. Wolfe, when did you find out about this supposed conspiracy between Ms. Melladin and me?"

"Just now. Jenny told me."

"Can you truly believe that Ms. Melladin could have arranged Captain Reading's death?"

A frown crossed Wolfe's even features. "I wouldn't have thought so, but —"

"I heard you fighting," said Hardin to Lyria. "He was going to fire you — so you came to Vron, and planned the whole thing so you could go on being Secretary."

Lyria said with sarcastic admiration, "You are really good at spinning lies — a new story for every occasion. What did you tell Ian? I can't believe he wanted to murder Bill. Ian, look at the way she lies. How could you trust her?"

"Mr. Wolfe," asked Vron, "who prevented you from getting to the meeting today?"

"Jenny did."

"And she was very insistent about it?"

"How did you — ? Are you reading my mind?"

"No," replied Vron. "But think — you were not supposed to arrive in time to rescue us. The alert mechanism blew with the power — how likely is that? No one was supposed to know until we were all dead. If Ms. Melladin and I had planned it, then Ms. Hardin must have been in conspiracy with us."

"Your lies are starting to trip you up, Jenny," said Lyria. "You convinced MacGregor you'd get him the Captaincy — but how long would he have it before you would be working on Ed Wolfe?" She turned to MacGregor. "Ian — she's young and ambitious. What would she get from your two or three years as Captain before you retired? Did you promise to make her your Secretary? How could you trust her after she got that position through conspiracy and murder?"

"Wait a minute!" said Wolfe. "Everybody's accusing everybody else. I don't know what to believe. Ian, Jenny, give me your weapons."

"Are you crazy?" demanded Hardin.

"No — I just want all four of you placed under security while I conduct an investigation."

"How do we know we can trust you?" she retorted. "You're next in line for Captain. You were the one who falsified Captain Reading's shuttle orbit!"

"Jenny." Ian MacGregor spoke slowly, painfully. "Jenny, what are you? I trusted you. I didn't know you were going to do murder and blame innocent people!"

"Shut up, Ian!"

"No. I can't stand any more." Tears slid down his face. "I've been a fool. Jenny came to me weeks ago, telling me I ought to be Captain. A young woman flattering an old man. I enjoyed it. She made me promise to make her my Secretary if I ever got my own Ship." He choked. "It was a game. All in fun."

"And then Captain Reading died," said Vron.

"I thought it was an accident!" said MacGregor, his eyes pleading.

"No!" cried Hardin. There was a click as she adjusted her weapon. Wolfe, beside her, saw the red "kill" setting light and grabbed for her arm.

She became a wildcat. Struggling with her, Wolfe could not fire his own weapon — and then hers fired, hitting MacGregor's right arm. He screamed and dropped his weapon as he fell, clutching burnt flesh.

Lyria ducked after MacGregor's weapon as it skittered across the floor, planning to stun Hardin — Wolfe too, if necessary. But Hardin would kill if she wasn't stopped.

Lyria groped for the weapon. Hardin fired again. Sparks sputtered as the shot burned away part of the wall.

The tank full of swarming insects set up a loud buzz. Hardin swung to see what it was, and Wolfe caught her gun arm, twisting it behind her back and wrenching the weapon away from her.

Vron bent over MacGregor. "He's alive. Call the medics."

Though the computer was still jammed, the intercom worked. Lyria called for security and a medical team, then turned back to the four figures by the door. Wolfe was holding Hardin, looking stunned. "I still don't know who did what."

"It's all here, Ed," said Lyria, picking up the sheaf of printouts.

"No!" gasped Hardin.

"Yes, Ms. Hardin — when you removed the privacy safeties you made it possible for Vron to record the evidence without either of us knowing it. Even if we find the program erased when we unjam the computer, we've got the printout, Ed — read it. Then you'll have the whole story."

"She," Wolfe shook Hardin, "she was going to kill you all today! And then go to work on me, I suppose!"

"Eventually," Lyria agreed. "But Ian would have survived today. The oxygen capsule he had with him at the board meeting is what led me to investigate further."

She looked at the crumpled form on the floor. MacGregor would probably lose his right arm. His involvement in murder and attempted murder would mean the end of his career. She could almost feel sorry for him, except

Lyria fought down tears. The medical and security teams took MacGregor and Hardin away. Wolfe took the sheaf of printouts. "I'll study these. Uh, you trust me with them? I'm not sure who to trust anymore!"

Vron said, "We must learn to trust one another again, Mr. Wolfe. If you can unjam a terminal, you might make certified copies, just in case. We will have a hearing at eight hundred hours tomorrow, and send the results to the Board of Directors."

"Right, Captain."

When everyone else had gone, Lyria started to leave, too. Vron said, "Ms. Melladin —"

Her control was eroding. "Please," she whispered, "I must go —" Her tears broke through her control. All her grief over Bill's death, held under numb disbelief for days, overcame her now. She stumbled toward the door. Vron blocked her way. "Let me go. I don't want you to see —"

"That you cared about Bill? I knew that. You must express your sorrow, Lyria, but not out there where the crew can see you. Come, sit down."

He led her to the bed, and pulled up his specially constructed chair beside it. Lyria's sobs came from the bottom of her soul. Vron handed her tissues, and sat down — watching her, she somehow understood, with sympathy rather than curiosity.

All the burden of her grief poured forth. Bill's death became a reality, as did the fact that she must live on without him. Such a senseless death — killed by a crazed young woman seeking advancement for herself and entangling a foolish old man in her plot. It was all so stupid!

When she had worn out the storm of her grief, she did not allow herself the luxury of crying for the sake of crying. With a few hard swallows, she dried her eyes, and returned to the knowledge that she was in Vron's cabin as she saw suspended over the bed a heavy wooden pole covered with claw marks. She remembered hearing that Arcadians rested by hanging from tree branches

Her new Captain was alien indeed, but not unfeeling, she realized as she sat up and dried her eyes. "I'm all right now. May I wash my face before I leave?"

"Of course."

When she came out of the lavatory, Vron was saying into the intercom, "I shall be in cargo hold seventeen. Do not disturb me except in case of emergency."

Hold seventeen was immense — and empty right now, Lyria recalled. Although she suspected the answer, she had to ask, "What are you going to do in the cargo hold?"

"I, too, cared about Bill Reading," he replied. "He was my friend; I feel sorrow at his death. My outlet for grief is different from yours, Lyria. At this time, I *must* fly."

She managed a watery smile. "And you can fly in zero gee in the cargo hold. Go, then. I'm sorry I kept you."

"No . . . you needed your release. We must understand such things about one another if we are to work together."

"Yes," agreed Lyria. "We can learn, I know. Go, now, and find your release. The *Venture* will be waiting for you when you return."

SHORT QUARTER

Edgar Wolfe sat watching and admiring a consummate artist at work. Lyria Melladin, Secretary of the CSS *Venture*, was busy telling a tale of woe that would convince Barth Hewitt, Captain of their sister ship, *Valor*, that everything was going fine.

"Of course the investigation of Bill's death, and the hearing, made us late with our first delivery of the quarter."

So we lost the order, thought Wolfe, and were stuck with a hold full of medical restraints.

"Then on Beranicus," Lyria continued, "we lost a sale of verimium tubing for the mines. Undercut by a ship out of Vega Seven — he said. The price he offered was 'way below what we had paid; we couldn't afford that kind of loss, so we let them buy from the pirate."

"Was he a pirate?" asked Hewitt.

"How can you sell below cost unless you steal the goods? But we were one on one, and not armed to take on a pirate ship. Beranicus is pretty far out of the regular lanes, so we decided it was best to leave, pretending we thought they were a legitimate business."

"Too bad," said Hewitt, his lined face a mask of false sympathy. Then sincerity took over as he said, "I guess I'd have done the same. I'm not ready to take on pirates. The corporations ought to get together and provide protection for their starships. But tell me — how are you getting along with your new Captain?"

"Just fine," said Wolfe, glad to contribute something he could say sincerely. He knew what Hewitt was fishing for: Vron was the first nonhuman the Corporation had ever given command of a Starship.

"He is doing an excellent job, under trying circumstances," Lyria added.

"But how about the crew? Do they accept him?"

"There was some difficulty at first."

Seven crew members jumped ship at Beranicus, Wolfe recalled, glad that there were no telepaths on the tavern terrace. "But everyone likes Vron," he added. "He's been on board for years, worked his way up to Chief Accountant, then First Vice-Chairman. It was the natural thing for the Board to promote him after Captain Reading was killed."

"The natural thing, eh?" said Hewitt, looking off somewhere behind Lyria and Wolfe. "Isn't that your Captain now?"

The plan had begun. As more and more people on the terrace caught sight of the Arcadian, chairs were turned to watch the show. Wolfe turned, too, and forgot everything in the breathtaking beauty of Vron in flight.

On board ship, Vron was an alien out of his element. His wings caught on things and in things, and knocked things over. Running down either side of his body, they prevented him from wearing ordinary clothing, as nothing could pass around his body. Up close, his almost featureless face seemed unreadable, expressionless.

Now, though, wings unfurled to catch the air currents, he was in his element. The sun shone on his golden-brown fur as he caught an updraft and soared, tumbling from the top by pulling his arms and legs in and plummeting toward the ground as the watchers gasped.

But well before he reached the ground he stretched out again, the wind billowing his wings as he lay motionless on the air, facing into the breeze. Gliding into the updraft again, he came down from it this time in a dizzying spiral.

At length, Wolfe remembered what the show was for, and tore his eyes from the display to look around. The attention of everyone on the terrace was riveted on the performance. In the town below, people stopped in the streets, and others came out of shops and houses to see what was happening. Some were hanging out of windows to see.

Oh, yes, it was working perfectly!

Vron continued his aerobatics for several minutes more. Finally, though, he made a last glide down into the open green below the tavern, landing on his feet. As he lowered his arms, his wings became capelike folds. A disappointed sigh rose from the watchers.

Captain Hewitt turned back to Lyria and Wolfe.

"Now there's something everyone would like to do. Too bad you can't bottle it and sell it."

"Yes, isn't it," purred Lyria, a mischievous gleam in her dark eyes that Wolfe hadn't seen since before Captain Reading's death.

Wolfe had been assigned to the *Venture* only two years ago, and made Vice-Chairman in charge of Sales last year. Everything had seemed to be going so smoothly, with Reading and Lyria running the ship efficiently at the same time that they were planning their personal union. The ship had been happily abuzz with wedding plans, until the sudden tragedy of Reading's murder.

It was a near-fatal blow to ship's morale. Wolfe had thought it might also be a death blow to the spirited side of Lyria's nature. For two months she had been polite, efficient . . . and empty. Seeing a flicker of her old self, Wolfe hoped desperately that their plan would work, so that the *Venture* crew would have a chance to settle into their new personnel structure and become a team.

As it was his plan, he felt very much concerned. Perhaps he felt kinship with Vron because each of them faced a test this quarter . . . and in a short quarter at that. If their plan to unload their cargo here on Monchresi didn't work, they would have to give a negative report. The Board would forgive a low profit under the circumstances. They had never been known to excuse a substantial loss.

Vron was clearly an experiment. There had been no other possibility for Captain except Lyria or Wolfe, but there was no one to take over Lyria's job as Secretary — and a ship could function more easily without a Captain than without a Secretary.

If the Board had refused to break precedent, Wolfe might have found himself in his first and last command. At twenty-four, he was a damn good sales executive. The premature promotion to First Vice-Chairman put him on the spot enough; he could only hope that he would grow into it fast enough not to jeopardize his career.

Lyria was a long proven, efficient Secretary; the Board would always find a place for her. But Vron and Wolfe were on the line now. If this plan did not result in the quick sale of slow moving cargo, they would both likely be out in the vacuum.

Wolfe was only half paying attention to Lyria and Hewitt. Vron was walking up the street toward the tavern, stopping along the way when people hailed him. He was used to that — a winged man was a rarity on most planets, and Vron flew wherever conditions allowed. For the thousandth time, Wolfe wondered why Vron had chosen to live in the confines of a starship . . . but he didn't know his Captain well enough to press beyond the evasive answers the Arcadian always gave to that question.

Vron strode gracefully up the center of the street. One forgot how incredibly graceful he was, until he was in a place with room to move. He was about the same size and shape as a human, but he was lighter, designed for flying. His weight, Wolfe had been surprised to discover, was less than half that of a human male of the same size. His bones were hollow, he had explained during the discussions of aerodynamics on the way here, his cells containing air pockets, and far less water than human cells.

Even so, he couldn't take off for flight from the ground; his species flew from tree to giant tree on their home planet, and required a height from which to begin soaring. He was therefore built to climb, too — Wolfe had once seen him go straight up the side of a building, using the heavy claws that served him as hands and feet to grasp every small point of leverage.

Wolfe waved to Vron from the terrace. Lyria turned, too, and beckoned to him.

Vron's answering wave sent a basket of flowers spilling from a passing pushcart. He stopped to set things right — then with two bounds and a vault he was on the terrace, holding his arms, and thus his wings, close to his sides as he threaded through the tables to where they sat.

"Captain Hewitt," he said in his musical voice. "How nice to see you again."

"Captain Vron," Hewitt acknowledged. "Congratulations on your promotion."

"Thank you," said Vron, choosing a very straight chair with a narrow back. He could not sit in contour chairs without pinching the delicate membranes of his wings. He continued to Hewitt, "I did not seek command, and certainly never wished to obtain it under these circumstances."

Wolfe wondered if Hewitt heard the sorrow behind those words, or if the Arcadian was to him still unreadably alien.

Hewitt was saying, "Your officers have been telling me you've had a rough quarter."

"Indeed," replied Vron, playing the game easily. "And a short quarter at that. The Board will not be pleased with our report. The three of us will prepare that report the next two days, while the crew takes shore leave."

"You're not going to claim you've come to MonkeySee for shore leave!" said Hewitt. "You won't pass up the opportunity to sell something."

"No, indeed," replied Vron. "Mr. Calloway has already set up a stand in the marketplace. What are we selling, Ed?"

"Oh, a few musical crystals, some Cytherean jewelry, Rornian silk — a lot of odds and ends," Wolfe replied casually.

Hewitt studied the three of them. "Too bad we've got to leave tomorrow. I'd love to know what you're really up to!"

*****

The next morning, after the last of the *Valor*'s shuttles had gone, the people of Monchresi — fondly known to corporation crews as MonkeySee — found out what the Venture was really up to. At mid-morning, as the resort town was bustling with activity, Vron appeared once more in the cloudless sky. Again people stopped to watch as he soared and dived, drifted and spun. This time, however, he did not remain alone.

Suddenly, from the top of the hill, five other flyers joined him — five great sail shapes in red, yellow, blue, green, and orange, riding the breeze, larger, slower, and more majestic than the tumbling Arcadian.

Following Vron's lead, they caught the updraft,

soared, spiraled out, swooped joyously upward once more, circled the valley, and landed in the open green below. There, human figures detached themselves from the great sails, while people poured from town toward the green, seeing that this was equipment with which they, themselves, could fly — and wanting it.

That was basic to the character of Monchresians: what they saw, they wanted. And, since their planet was rich in the lichtenium necessary to power the warp drive of the giant starships, they could have anything money could buy.

The trick now was to ride the wave of immediate enthusiasm, and sell out the hundreds of hang gliders the Venture's crew had constructed from the lightweight verimium tubing, and the restraining straps and heavy everything proof sheeting originally intended for the hospital planet, Regulus II. When their late delivery cost them that order, it had seemed they would be stuck with expensive, highly specialized supplies, until Wolfe had come up with the idea of selling their Captain's ability to fly.

Wolfe had done gliding at college on Sornium — and watching Vron had brought out the yearning to get up there again. The Monchresians felt the same yearning; the gliders were snapped up as quickly as they could be unloaded from the shuttles and bolted together.

Wolfe, and the four others with some experience, spent the day on the hilltop, instructing new enthusiasts and directing traffic, lest too many inexperienced flyers be in the air at once. By evening,

Wolfe was hoarse, aching, and dead tired — but hopeful. They had sold his glider out from under — or over — him, so he had to trudge down the hill when the sun set.

The Monchresians had a high level of technology, all imported since the discovery of lichtenium. Wolfe didn't even stop to find out how much money they had taken in, but went straight to his hotel room, turned on the holographic display, and drew a hot bath, a luxury every hotel that catered to starship crews provided. A ship's vibra-showers might get a man cleaner than water, but they certainly didn't provide the warmth and comfort.

The hologram followed him while he soaked and stretched his muscles. He had tuned to the news channel, hoping to see the last requirement of their scheme. They had to sell in quantity, not merely the two hundred or so they had sold today in one town, and they had to do it tomorrow, so their quarterly report could be sent the next day.

The warm, soothing water almost put him to sleep before the item he was hoping for came on the air. But there it was! There he was, on the planetwide news. There was Vron, followed by the gliders. Wolfe was flying the blue one, clearly having a good time. It had been great to get up there again.

The news story told who they were, and where. *That does it!* thought Wolfe happily. Within a week, enterprising Monchresians would be manufacturing their own versionsbut some bright merchant would be here first, to grab up the Venture's supply and make a quick profit before a local imitation could be ready.

Wolfe had almost fallen asleep in the tub, when there was a pounding at the door. With a start, he hopped out, pulled on an absorbent robe, and called "Come in!" to the servomechanism.

As he went out to the main room, Vron and Lyria entered.

"Did you see it?" asked Lyria. "It worked! Congratulations."

"A good job indeed," said Vron. "Two distributors called immediately after the broadcast; one will pick up fifty gliders tomorrow, and the other wants to come and try them before he decides — but he asked if we could provide a thousand."

"We can!" said Wolfe. "How many do we have left?"

"1,532. If we sell that thousand, we shall have a small profit to report."

"This calls for a drink!" said Wolfe. He had a bottle of Womican brandy. As Vron accepted his drink, he cocked his head to one side, looking Wolfe up and down. "You're wet."

"You got me out of the bathtub."

Vron shuddered. "How can you stand to soak yourself in water?"

"To us it feels good," laughed Lyria. "We'll have to take you swimming sometime, Vron."

"No, thank you!"

Their teasing mood was broken by the message chime, and a voice paging Vron. "I wonder what now?" Wolfe said, as Vron responded to the holographic player.

The image solidified again — Captain Barth Hewitt. However, his message was indecipherable, the image jerking and twitching, the sound garbled nonsense.

"Scrambled," said Lyria. "Do you think one of us should go up to the ship to decode it, Captain?"

"It could be urgent," said Vron. "Lyria, can you decode it on this unit without being tapped?"

"Sure" she replied. "It's a standard holovision." She removed the cover, and the image disappeared as her quick fingers played among the interior components. Wolfe could have done it, and he thought Vron might be able to — but it would have taken them hours, and he wasn't sure he could trust himself to create an effective firewall if an expert of Lyria's capability were trying to tap it.

"There," she said after less than ten minutes, snapping the cover into place. She pressed a button, and the hologram showed a hovering blue sphere. "No bugs in the room. We can play it safely."

*****

As it turned out, the scramble was not to conceal it from anyone on Monchresi. Hewitt's statement was brief: "Just passed a strange ship on its way to MonkeySee. It refused our hail, and the description tallies with your friend from Beranicus. Take care — a sale isn't worth a fight. Message ends."

Wolfe laughed. "I doubt they have gliders aboard — and we don't care how cheap they sell anything else they've stolen!"

"I don't like it," said Lyria. "That's a bold pirate to come to MonkeySee. Corporation ships are constantly in and out."

"They probably won't land where we are," said Vron. "We'll be here one more day. I'm sure Captain

Hewitt will pass the word to other ships, and so shall we."

Wolfe said, "If it's the same pirate, he didn't do anything but undersell us on Beranicus. There's no reason to think he'll bother us here."

He was partly right. The pirates ignored the Venture party, landing on the other side of the planet at the capital city.

Wolfe was back on the hilltop at noon the next day, instructing individual buyers, while Vron negotiated with the distributor for the sale of the thousand gliders that would put them in the black. Suddenly his transceiver beeped. He thumbed it on, and Lyria's voice, calm but concerned, said, "Come down to the hotel, Ed. We've got trouble."

He turned the woman he was instructing over to Calloway, strapped himself into a glider, and wafted down to the green.

The mayor of the town was in Vron's room, explaining what had happened: the pirates, accepted in the capital as legitimate traders, had gone to show the President what they claimed was a marvelous new product. Instead, they had produced weapons and taken hostage the President, his wife, and his daughter, carrying them off in a shuttle.

"We ask you, Captain, to use your ship, your crew, against these evil traders," said the mayor. "They are your own people; you must take the responsibility."

"They're not our people," Wolfe protested.

Vron shook his head at him. "The corporations have attracted all kinds of people to Monchresi," he said. "This ship is certainly not a legitimate trader.

However, we are not armed for battle. We have only a few hand weapons aboard. Even if we could attack, your President might be harmed."

"I have been instructed by the Council," the mayor said stiffly, "to inform you that all trade with any corporation ship ceases from this moment, until our President is safely released to us. Dorom, you hear that?"

"Yes, Your Honor," replied the Monchresian trader reluctantly. The deal must not have been concluded before the interruption.

"We'll help if we can," said Vron. "Your Honor, have the kidnapers said why they've taken your President?"

They were demanding a ransom, it seemed — 5,000 kilos of lichtenium. That amount would wipe out Monchresi's stockpile, making it impossible to meet the demands of corporation starships for months. The pirates would be able to sell their supply at inflated prices — or withhold it as a power play, as trading ships had to have lichtenium to use their warp drives.

When Vron and the two humans were alone once more, Lyria asked, "How do we go about rescuing the President?"

"We are all agreed that we must attempt it?" asked Vron.

Wolfe shrugged. "What else can we do? It's not just our own sales — that hardly compares to Mon-keySee's cutting off trade with all the corporations. More important, those pirates have three innocent people who might be hurt — even killed — if they don't get what they want."

"The Monchresians don't understand violence," said Lyria. "They have no army, no police force, and no idea of how to handle a situation like this."

"And the corporations, by opening trade on this planet, opened Monchresi to piracy," added Vron. "Very well. The first thing we must find out is where they took the President."

"To their ship, of course," said Wolfe.

"I think not. Richardson's been scanning from the *Venture* since the kidnapping, and no shuttle has approached the pirate vessel."

"I wonder why?" said Wolfe. "It would seem the safest place."

"Removing persons from their native planet for criminal purposes?" said Lyria. "It would mean an automatic death sentence for everyone involved. It seems they do care something for Intragalactic Law."

"Then they won't want to kill anyone, either," Wolfe said hopefully.

"Unless we make them panic," cautioned Lyria. "I think we can assume they don't want to harm the President or his family — or move them off planet. So we must find out where they are."

That took only three hours. One of the Venture shuttles found a power trace, swooped in to investigate, and was shot at.

"Missed us by a kilometer, and gave themselves away," reported Benrum, the *Venture*'s Vergian Chief Navigator. "I don't think they can have very much experience at this sort of crime."

Wolfe noted the confusion in the blue kewpie

doll face — Vergians found it difficult to conceive of dishonesty. They were the best navigators in the galaxy — and the worst salesmen.

Vron placed shuttles out of range of the pirates, ringing them in. He, Wolfe, and Lyria manned one of them, scouting the mountainous area in which the pirates were hiding.

"Now, how do we get in there?" asked Wolfe. "They're shooting at everything in range."

"If we had time," said Vron, "we could wait until several more corporation ships arrived, take their ship, and make a trade. However. . . ."

"Yeah, however," Wolfe agreed. They could not sit here doing nothing while the Monchresians closed down trade. Not to mention their own predicament, which had to be resolved today. The short quarter again — the problem of relativity that had given them only ten weeks, subjective time, while thirteen weeks passed on Earth. "We've got to go in, if we can get past the heavy artillery. We've got plenty of hand weapons."

"After dark I could fly in," said Vron. "Shuttle scanners pick up power sources, not living beings."

"You're not going in there alone!" said Lyria.

"I'll go with you," said Wolfe. "The gliders are unpowered."

"You can't see in the dark."

"I can with infrared goggles. It's just one shuttle with three spaces taken up by the hostages. Probably not more than ten pirates. There are five of us good with the gliders — and Benrum. He picked it up yesterday as if he'd been born to it."

"Vergians can navigate anything," said Lyria.

"Now I wish I'd let you talk me into learning to fly one of those."

"You're needed to pilot the shuttle," said Wolfe. "You'll have to come in after us."

"Seven of us," said Vron. "At most, ten of them — and we have the advantage of surprise. Yes — we'll do it!"

They didn't broadcast their plans, of course — shuttles were not equipped for scrambling. Thus they had to go around to each of the other shuttles, land, and parley. By nightfall they were in position, five humans and a Vergian with their gliders, and Vron.

The pirates were atop a bluff, almost impossible to reach on foot — and of course they assumed their scanners would show a power trail from anything approaching by air. The Venture shuttle landed just out of scanner range, where they bolted together the gliders for the expedition. When all were ready, Wolfe passed out the weapons, set to stun. He snapped his into the holster on his belt, but was interested to see Vron tuck his beneath the front of the garment he wore.

The Arcadian could not wear a belt, of course. His single piece of clothing was a contoured strip of cloth passing from a neckband, down his body and between his legs, up the back to the neckband again. "You're sure that's a safe place to carry a gun?" Wolfe asked.

"Oh, very safe," Vron replied. "I've got a pouch in there."

Smart, thought Wolfe, who often cursed the lack of pockets in the jumpsuits the Corporation provided.

As soon as it was full dark, they tumbled off the bluff to catch the air currents still rising from the rock warmed by the day's sunlight.

The infrared goggles made the night a crazy quilt world of colors, showing clearly where the warm, glowing updrafts were, contrasted to the cool, dark downdrafts.

They soared silently across the valley, carefully coming in below the bluff, so as not to be caught in the lantern light of the group of pirates. Wolfe caught only a distant glimpse, but thought there were not many pirates. Three figures huddled forlornly together had to be the President and his family.

Circling the bluff, they sought a landing place where they could ditch the gliders and approach on foot — in the air they made only too perfect targets. Vron took the lead in finding a spot where they all had room to land.

Benrum, with his perfect sense of direction, led them on foot toward the pirates' shuttle and the small group of figures outside it. They crept up quietly, and Wolfe saw the President, with his wife and daughter on either side of him, facing two armed pirates.

A third was in the shuttle, watching the scanner. Five others were eating, while a sixth patrolled just outside the circle of light.

Calloway leaned toward Wolfe and whispered, "Let's get the guard."

Wolfe nodded.

The two men waited on either side of the pirate's path. One hit high and one hit low, and they took him down silently — but not out. He got out a strangled gasp. It was enough.

"Feeny!" shouted one of the other pirates. When there was no answer, all but the ones guarding the hostages leaped up, drawing their weapons.

The Venture crew were anything but trained soldiers. Nonetheless, they acted almost as a man, seeing that the moment must be taken or their advantage lost.

Weapons out, they charged the pirates, duplicating effort here and leaving openings there — at least four of them stunned the guards covering the President's family, but three Venture crewmen dropped in their tracks as the other pirates shot them.

Wolfe went after the shuttle, and found the door sealed. He could see the woman inside making a call. His hand weapon would not penetrate the hull, but —

The idea was right, but too late. While he was resetting his weapon to destruct, and then shooting the antenna off the shuttle, the woman was taking off. He aimed for the power unit — too late.

He dived out of the way as the little craft was up and away amidst shouts of anger from the other pirates at their comrade's panicked move. Wolfe turned back to the fray just in time to help Vron, Benrum, and Calloway take advantage of the pirates' distraction.

"All right," said Benrum, imitating a law officer from the holovision shows, "we've got you covered. Throw down your weapons and you won't be hurt."

The tough words coming from a Vergian heightened the absurdity of the situation. The blue-skinned, potbellied Vergian hardly came up to Wolfe's shoulder, but he held his weapon steady, with an air of authority.

The four pirates left standing looked at one another, at their weapons, and at the motley crew surrounding them. Behind Benrum, the President got up, moving slowly, picked up a weapon from one of the fallen guards, and pointed it at the pirates. "Now you are outnumbered," he said. "Will you surrender?"

Wolfe suspected the Monchresian would not know what button to push — but the pirates either didn't know that, or didn't want to take the chance. They dropped their weapons.

Tension drained from Wolfe, and he found his legs shaking. God, what a muddle! If these pirates had been a well-organized, experienced band. . . .

Stunned combatants on both sides were beginning to stir as Vron pulled his transceiver out and said, "Lyria, we've got the President and his family safe. Come get them, and tell Reynolds to pick up the pirates. Did you see the other shuttle?"

"Yes," Wolfe heard her reply. "Richardson reports it rendezvoused with the ship. The *Valor* is back — they called the *Wanderer* from Concorp to help take the pirate vessel."

The shuttle was there almost before Lyria finished her message. From that point, the night was a blur to Wolfe. He remembered flashes: the President of Monchresi and his family embracing one another and crying; Benrum trembling so hard once it was all over that he had to be taken in Lyria's shuttle; the captured pirates vying to accuse one another of the kidnap plan; the report that the pirate ship had surrendered when outnumbered three to one.

At dawn Wolfe found himself, limbs rubbery and eyes scratchy, back at the hotel with Vron and Lyria. The Secretary sighed. "We won the most important part," she said. "The President and his family are safe, and that particular bunch of pirates are out of commission."

"Yeah," said Wolfe. "Maybe the Board will take that into consideration." He yawned. "At this point I almost don't care if I do lose my job."

"We can always become mercenary soldiers," said Vron.

It took Wolfe a moment, in his befuddled state, to realize that his Captain was joking. "Or pirates," he agreed. "Surely we could do a better job than the ones we just captured!"

Lyria and Wolfe laughed. Vron made a trilling sound deep in his throat, that Wolfe decided must be Arcadian laughter. He had never heard it before.

"Well, I'm off to bed," he said.

"Not until we file our report," replied Vron.

"Oh, no," Wolfe groaned. "Damn relativity anyway! Short quarters are against the laws of nature!"

Just then the message chime rang. When Vron responded, Dorom, the Monchresian merchant, appeared holographically. "At your convenience, Captain, I would like to conclude our transaction. May I make an appointment for later today, when you are rested?"

Vron glanced at the chronometer beneath the hologram. "Can you make it now, sir?"

"Yes, certainly. I'll be right up."

The image disappeared. Vron said, "Never damn relativity, Ed. If we can make this sale within the hour, board the *Venture*, and warp at top speed toward Earth, the same law that gave us a short quarter will give us the extra hour or so we'll need to get the report in — showing a profit."

"Yes, sir!" replied Wolfe. "Shall I relay your orders to the ship, Captain?"

"Yes, indeed. And round up the crew for immediate departure. Lyria, settle our hotel bill, then come back here to witness the transaction. Tell Benrum —"

The Captain was still issuing orders as Wolfe left to carry his out. Despite his weariness, he felt wonderful. Events on Monchresi might have shown that the crew of the Venture made a wretched showing as a fighting team — but as a sales team they were good and getting better. The feeling of camaraderie was back. Laughter was back. They had survived this quarter — and next quarter they would thrive!

ABOUT JEAN LORRAH

Jean Lorrah, the sole author of most of these stories, frequently collaborates with Jacqueline Lichtenberg, who edited this collection, and Lois Wickstrom, co-author of "The Rooster Under the Table."

Jean lives in Kentucky, and has a cat, Dudley, who is at least as well-known in her community as Jean is. Dudley is a therapy cat who walks on a leash, visits patients in nursing homes, participates in Humane Society activities at various events, and even walks in parades.

Jean has had more than twenty novels published over the years, and has recently begun writing screenplays as well. Find Jean's latest news at www.jeanlorrah.com.

www.ingramcontent.com/pod-product-compliance
Lightning Source LLC
Chambersburg PA
CBHW020651180626
46816CB00003B/1237